Spider-Man Presents The

MARVEL

JOKE BOOK

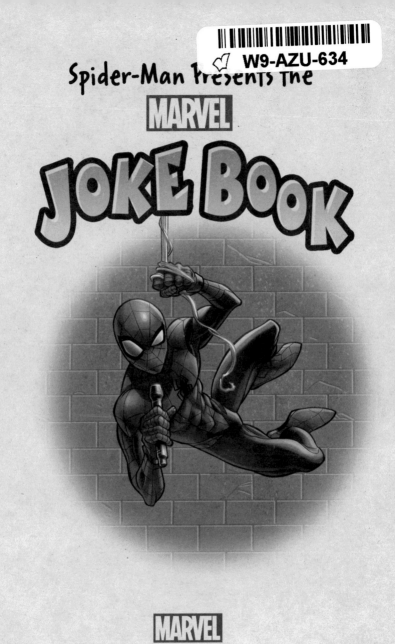

MARVEL

Los Angeles
New York

MARVEL
marvelkids.com

 For information address Marvel Press, 125 West End Avenue, New York, New York 10023.
Printed in the United States of America
First Paperback Edition, June 2017
10 9 8 7 6 5 4 3 2 1
Library of Congress Control Number: 2017935864
ISBN 978-1-368-00066-6
FAC-025438-17111

SUSTAINABLE FORESTRY INITIATIVE
Certified Chain of Custody
Promoting Sustainable Forestry
www.sfiprogram.org
SFI-01054
The SFI label applies to the text stock

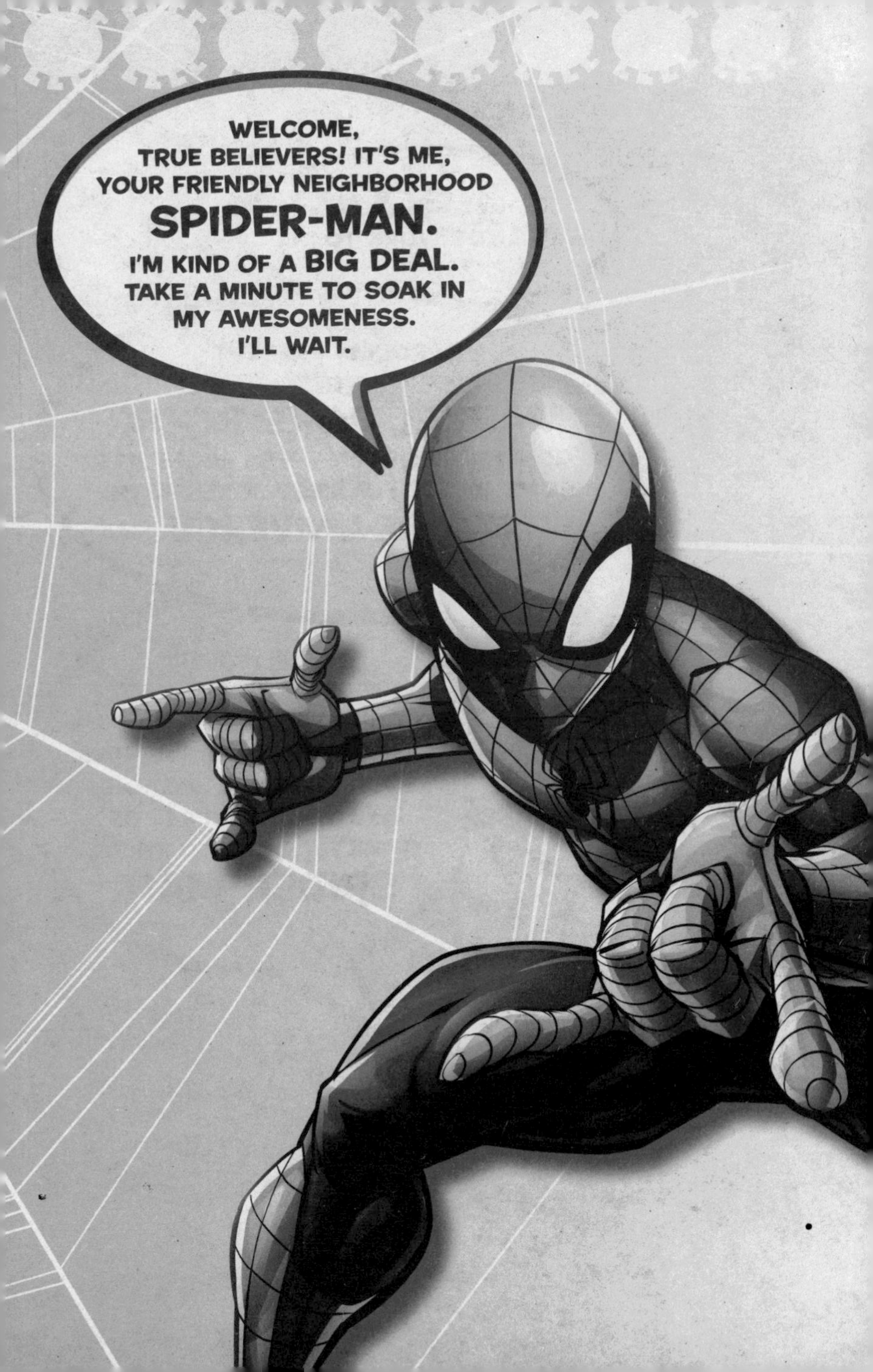
WELCOME, TRUE BELIEVERS! IT'S ME, YOUR FRIENDLY NEIGHBORHOOD SPIDER-MAN. I'M KIND OF A BIG DEAL. TAKE A MINUTE TO SOAK IN MY AWESOMENESS. I'LL WAIT.

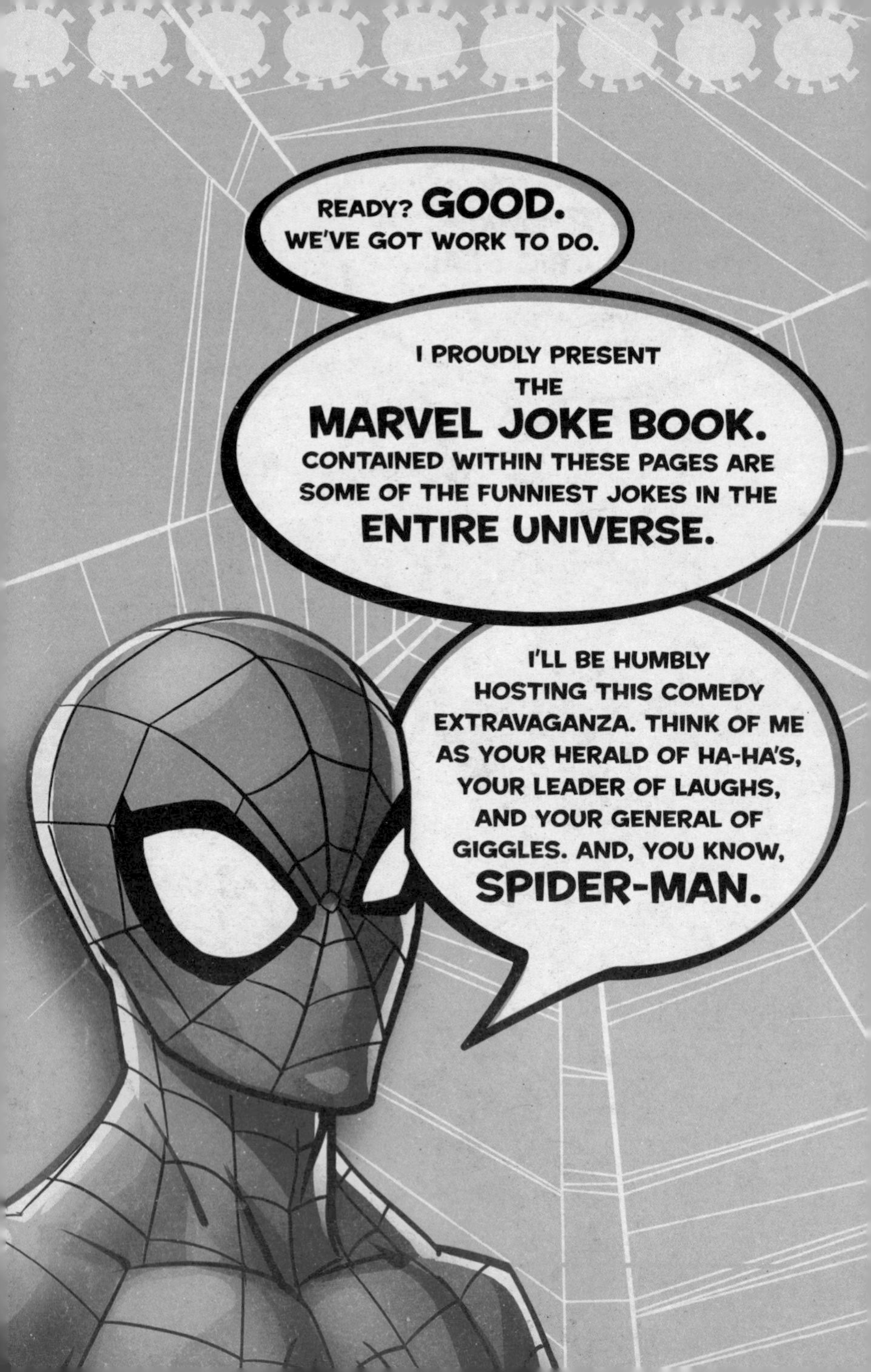
READY? GOOD. WE'VE GOT WORK TO DO.
I PROUDLY PRESENT THE MARVEL JOKE BOOK. CONTAINED WITHIN THESE PAGES ARE SOME OF THE FUNNIEST JOKES IN THE ENTIRE UNIVERSE.
I'LL BE HUMBLY HOSTING THIS COMEDY EXTRAVAGANZA. THINK OF ME AS YOUR HERALD OF HA-HA'S, YOUR LEADER OF LAUGHS, AND YOUR GENERAL OF GIGGLES. AND, YOU KNOW, SPIDER-MAN.

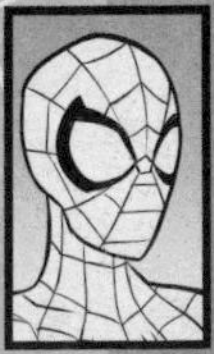

I'M HERE TO TURN **YOU** INTO A WORLD-CLASS COMEDIAN. WE'LL START WITH THE BASICS AND THEN . . . LET'S JUST SAY, BY THE TIME THIS IS ALL OVER YOU'LL BE A LEAN, MEAN JOKE MACHINE. **BUCKLE UP, BUTTERCUP!** GET READY TO LEARN FROM THE BEST—ME!

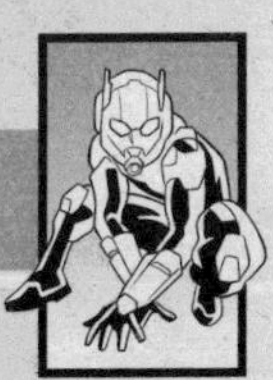

Oh, like we're supposed to follow you because you're a comedy genius or something?

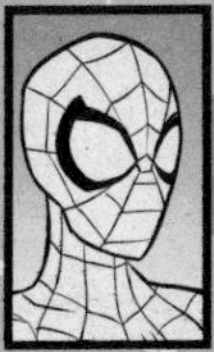

YES. **NOW BEAT IT, ANT-BOY!**

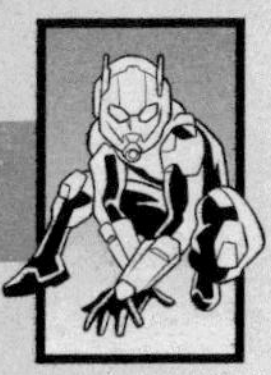

The name is Ant-Man. **ANT-MAN.**

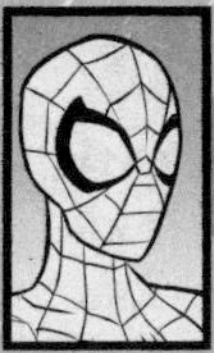

GO AWAY. IT'S NOT YOUR TIME YET!

HOW TO TELL A JOKE

**COMEDY COMES IN MANY DIFFERENT FORMS.
THE MOST COMMON FORM IS**
THE JOKE!

**HERE ARE SOME TIPS ON HOW
TO TELL A GOOD JOKE.**

Step #1: Choose a joke

**FIND A JOKE THAT YOU THINK IS FUNNY. THAT WAY
YOU'LL LOVE TELLING IT TO PEOPLE.**

Step #2: Figure it out

JOKES HAVE TWO THINGS: A SET-UP AND A PUNCH LINE.

Example:
Q: What happens when a banana gets a sunburn?

**THIS IS THE SETUP. IT PRESENTS THE IDEA OF THE JOKE
AND GETS YOUR AUDIENCE THINKING ABOUT WHAT
THE ANSWER MIGHT BE.**

A: It peels!

**THIS IS THE PUNCH LINE. IT'S WHERE YOU GET THE
LAUGHS! IT'S SURPRISING AND FUN. IT CAN ALSO MAKE
PEOPLE THINK.**

Step #3: Prepare

REHEARSE YOUR JOKE! YOU WANT TO MAKE SURE YOU TELL IT AWESOMELY.

Step #4: Perform

CHOOSE AN AUDIENCE, LIKE A FRIEND OR FAMILY MEMBER. DON'T TELL THEM YOU'RE ABOUT TO LAY DOWN SOME HYSTERICAL HUMOR. NO NEED TO BE NERVOUS, EITHER—YOU'VE GOT THIS! SPEAK CLEARLY AND, MOST IMPORTANTLY, HAVE FUN.

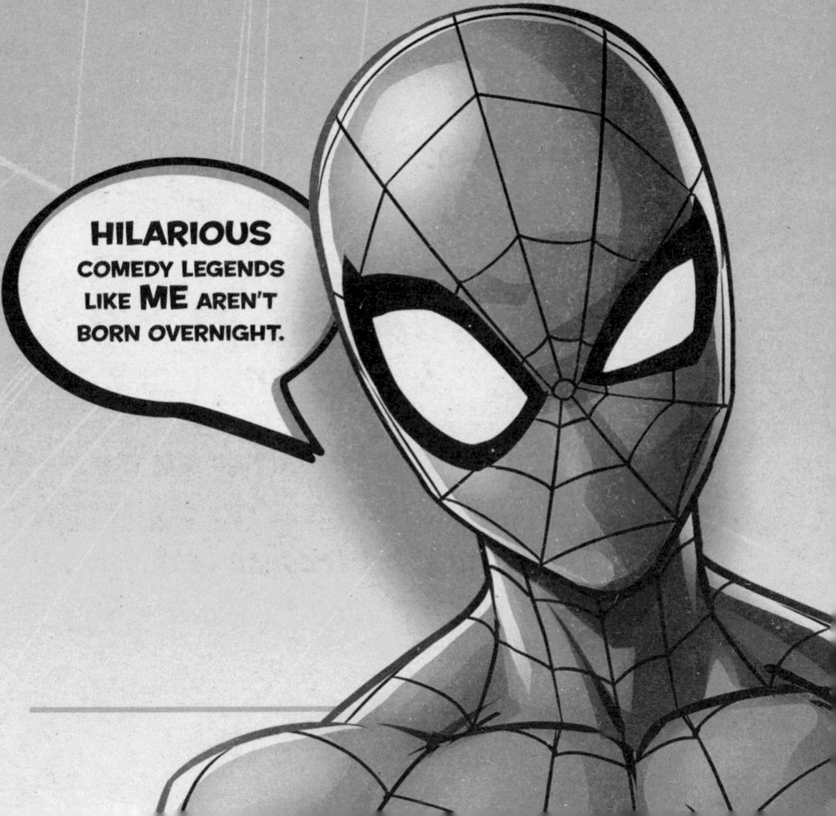
HILARIOUS COMEDY LEGENDS LIKE ME AREN'T BORN OVERNIGHT.

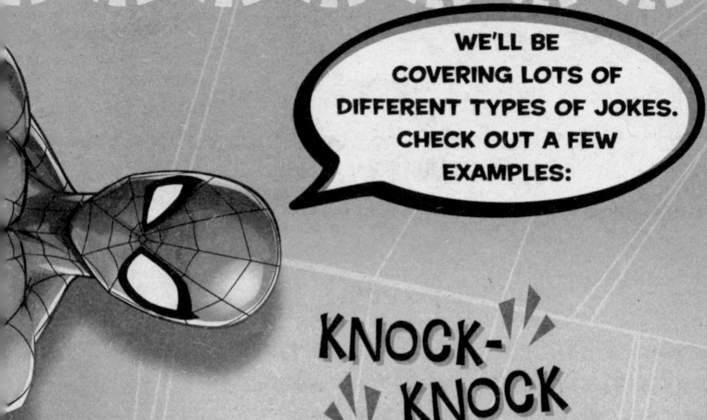
WE'LL BE COVERING LOTS OF DIFFERENT TYPES OF JOKES. CHECK OUT A FEW EXAMPLES:

KNOCK-KNOCK

Knock, knock.

Who's there?

Radio.

Radio who?

Radio not, here we go!

Questions & Answers

Q: Why did Peter Parker eat his math homework?

A: Because his teacher said it was a piece of cake.

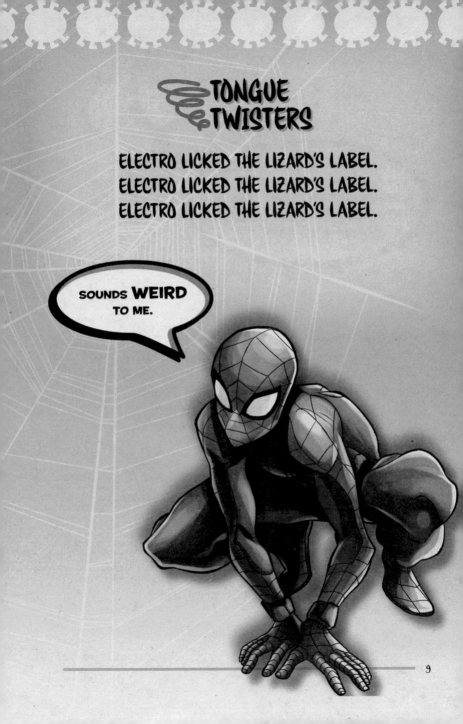

TONGUE TWISTERS

ELECTRO LICKED THE LIZARD'S LABEL.
ELECTRO LICKED THE LIZARD'S LABEL.
ELECTRO LICKED THE LIZARD'S LABEL.

SOUNDS **WEIRD** TO ME.

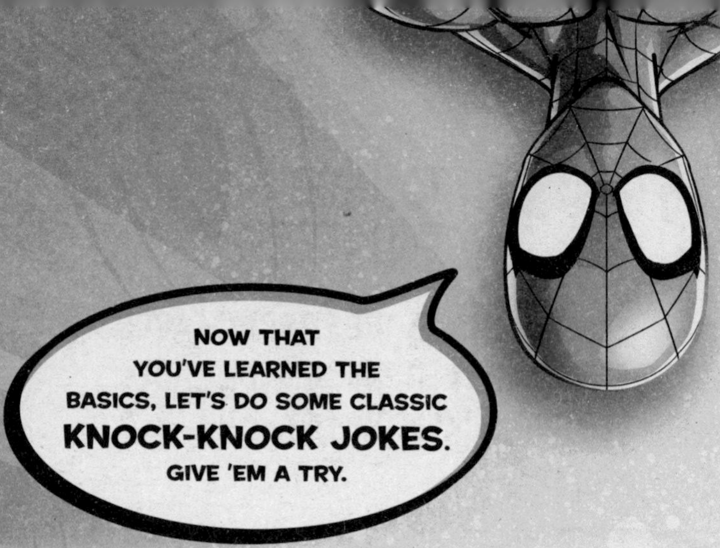
NOW THAT YOU'VE LEARNED THE BASICS, LET'S DO SOME CLASSIC KNOCK-KNOCK JOKES. GIVE 'EM A TRY.

Knock, knock.
Who's there?
Nun.
Nun who?
Nun of your business.

Knock, knock.
Who's there?
Meyer.
Meyer who?
Meyer nosy.

Knock, knock.
Who's there?
Pecan.
Pecan who?
Pecan somebody your own size!

Knock, knock.
Who's there?
Zany.
Zany who?
Zany body in there?

Knock, knock.
Who's there?
Fairy.
Fairy who?
Fairy nice to meet you, I'm Spider-Man!

Knock, knock.
Who's there?
Lena.
Lena who?
Lena little bit closer, and I'll tell you.

Knock, knock.
Who's there?
Dare.
Dare who?
Dare must be some mistake, you're in my house!

Knock, knock.
Who's there?
Penny.
Penny who?
Penny for your thoughts?

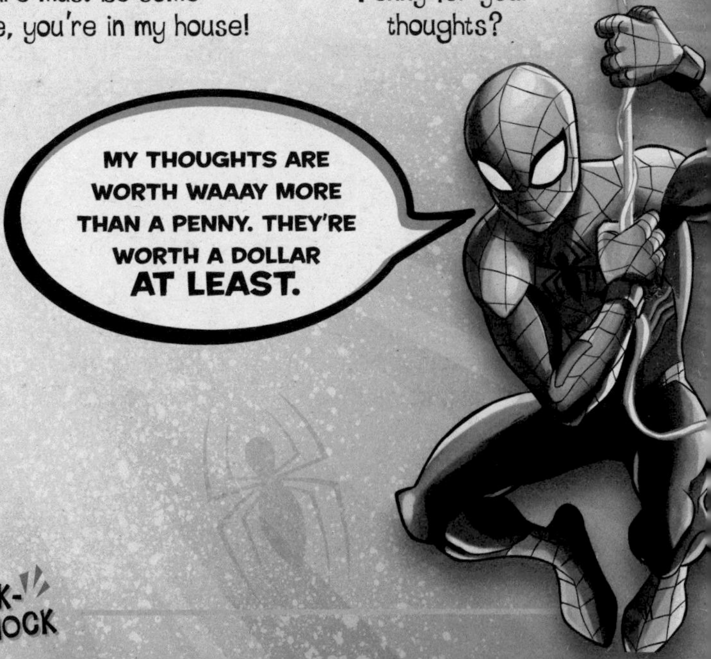
MY THOUGHTS ARE WORTH WAAAY MORE THAN A PENNY. THEY'RE WORTH A DOLLAR AT LEAST.

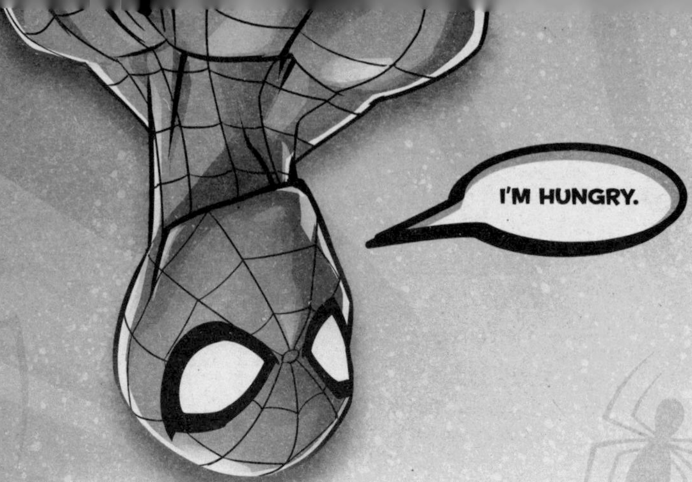
I'M HUNGRY.

Knock, knock.
Who's there?
Noah.
Noah who?
Noah good place to get a slice of pizza around here? I'm starving.

Knock, knock.
Who's there?
Stan.
Stan who?
Stan back! I'm knocking this door down!

Knock, knock.
Who's there?
Rita.
Rita who?
Rita book sometime. You might learn something.

Knock, knock.
Who's there?
Dots.
Dots who?
Dots for me to know and you to find out.

Knock, knock.
Who's there?
Juicy.
Juicy who?
Juicy what I just saw?

Knock, knock.
Who's there?
Jamaica.
Jamaica who?
Jamaica great lasagna!

Knock, knock.
Who's there?
Wooden shoe.
Wooden shoe who?
Wooden shoe like to know?

Knock, knock.
Who's there?
Weird.
Weird who?
Weird you hide the chocolate?!

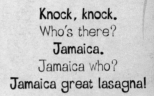

I'M GETTING SUPER HUNGRY NOW.

KNOCK-KNOCK

13

WHEN THE TEACHER CALLS ON YOU AND YOU GOTTA ACT LIKE YOU'RE THINKIN' ABOUT THE ANSWER

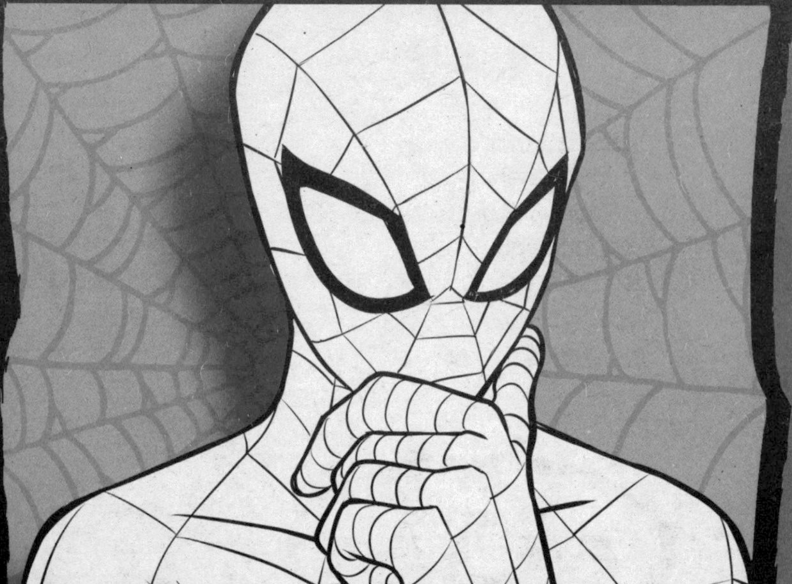

BUT REALLY YOU'VE BEEN ASLEEP FOR THE PAST HOUR AND A HALF

TIME FOR SOME
**QUESTIONS &
ANSWERS!**

???

Q: What do you call a rude cow with a twitch?
A: Beef jerky.

???

Q: Why are spiders like toy tops?
A: They are always spinning!

???

Q: What is a Super Hero's favorite part
of the joke?
A: The "punch" line!

???

Q: What has two legs but can't walk?
A: A pair of pants.

Q: What breaks when Spider-Man
starts talking?
A: The silence.

???

Q: What is a Super Hero's favorite drink?
A: Fruit punch!

???

Q: What do you call a pig with three eyes?
A: A piiig.

???

Q: What do you call a snowman's parents?
A: Mom and Popsicle.

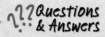

???

Q: What does a Super Hero put
in their drink?
A: Just ice.

???

Q: Why did the baby cookie cry?
A: Because its mom was a wafer so long.

???

Q: What kind of songs are
balloons afraid of?
A: Pop songs.

???

Q: Why did the teacher wear glasses?
A: Because her class was so bright.

HOW'S IT GOING?
FEELING GOOD?
FEELING LIKE A
COMEDIAN
YET?

???

Q: What is Spider-Man's favorite
kind of rice?
A: **Sticky rice!**

???

Q: Why did the potato cross the road?
A: **It saw a fork up ahead.**

???

Q: What did Iron Man get for
acting up in class?
A: **De-TIN-tion!**

???

Q: What type of key opens a banana?
A: **A mon-key.**

ME: I'M THE HARDEST WORKER. MY BOSS LOVES ME. I DESERVE A RAISE!

ALSO ME, AT WORK:

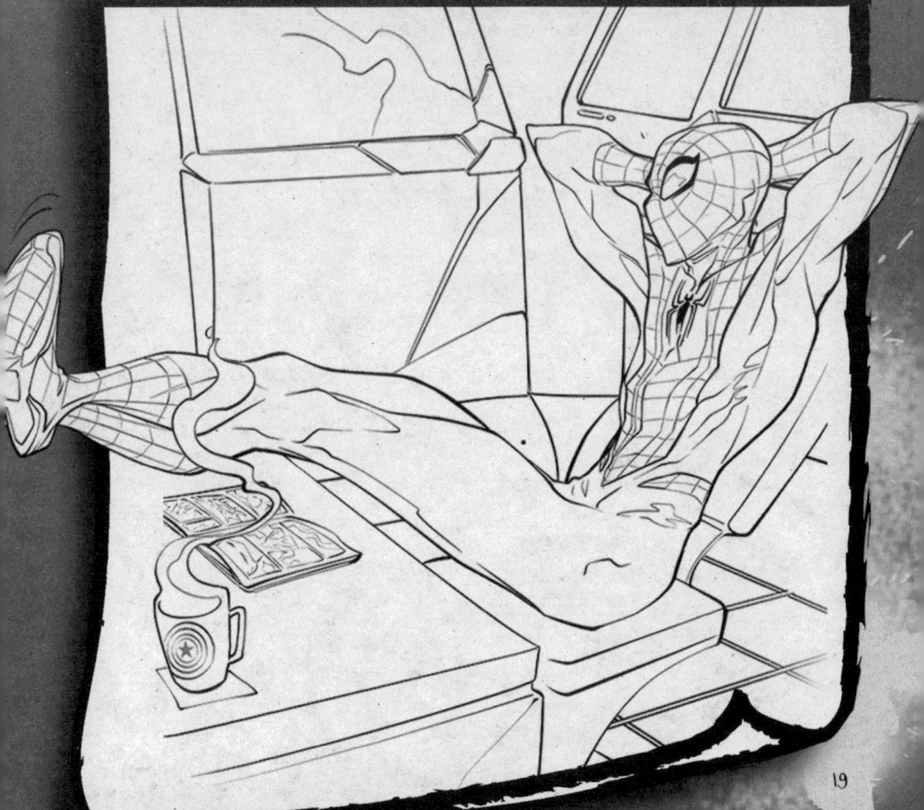

Q: What's Peter Parker's nighttime job?
A: He's a web designer.

Q: What does Spider-Man eat
with a cheeseburger?
A: French flies!

Q: What do you call
an undercover spider?
A: A spy-duuuurr!

Q: What do you call Spider-Man and his new
wife right after they get married?
A: Newly webs.

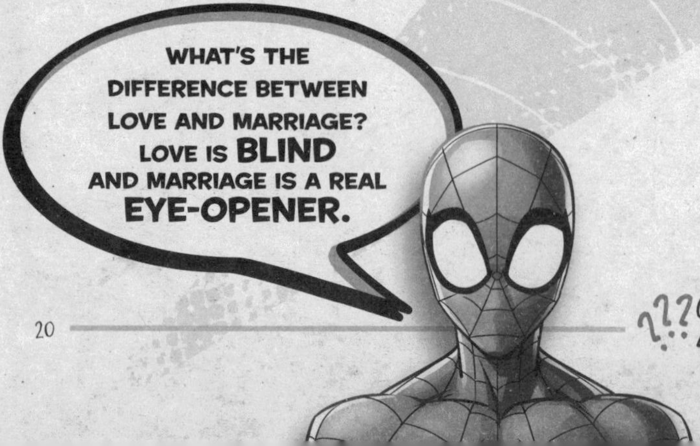
WHAT'S THE DIFFERENCE BETWEEN LOVE AND MARRIAGE? LOVE IS BLIND AND MARRIAGE IS A REAL EYE-OPENER.

Q: Where does Spider-Man go to find information?

A: The World Wide Web.

Q: Why is Spider-Man a good baseball player?

A: He knows how to catch flies!

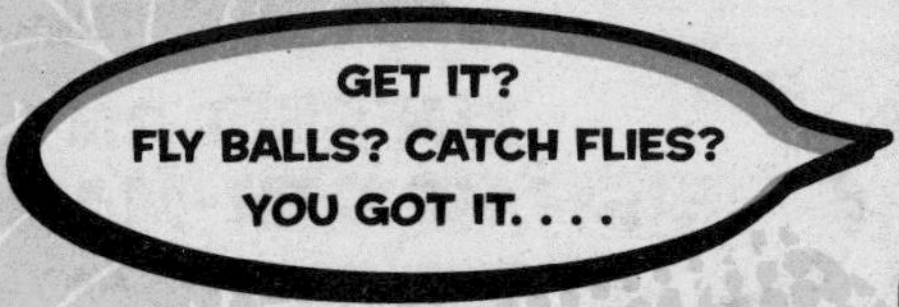
GET IT?
FLY BALLS? CATCH FLIES?
YOU GOT IT. . . .

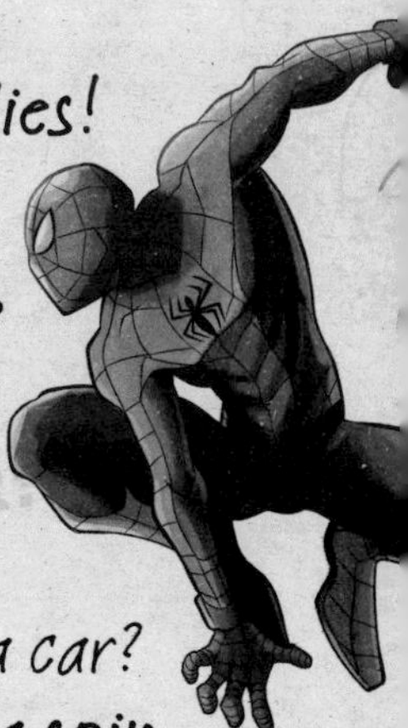

Q: Why did Spider-Man rent a car?

A: So he could take it out for a spin.

Q: Did you hear about Spider-Man's love life?

A: It's a very tangled web.

???

Q: What do you call the Irish Spider-Man?
A: Paddy Longlegs!

THERE'S AN IRISH SPIDER-MAN?!?!
SOMEBODY CALL MY LAWYER.

???

Q: What's Spider-Man's favorite dance?
A: The jitterbug.

???

Q: Why did Spider-Man join the swim team?
A: Because he had webbed feet.

???Questions
& Answers

COSTUME PATROL

THWIP OR THWOP?

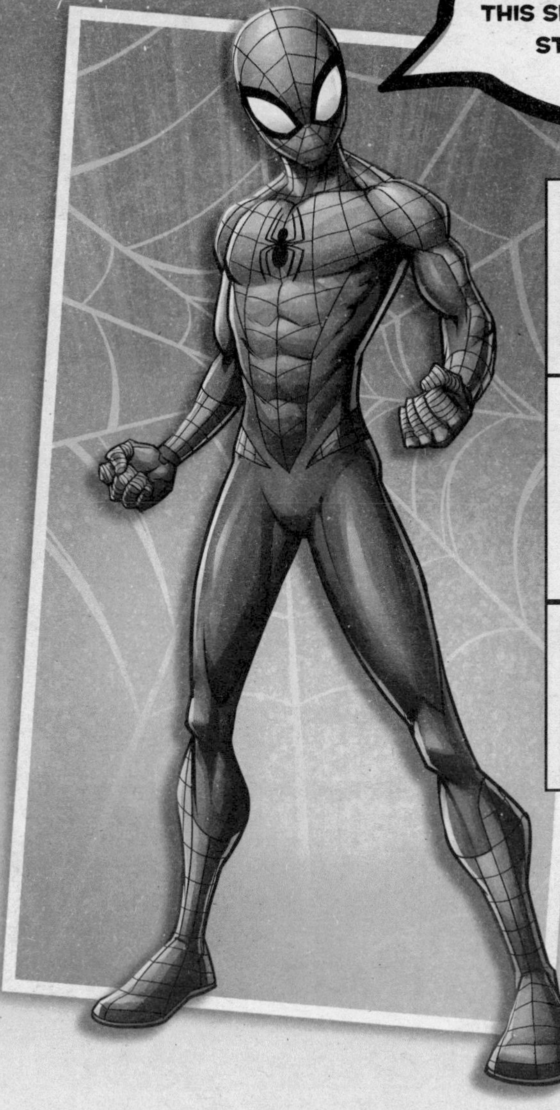
HOLD UP JUST ONE MINUTE. I DID NOT OKAY THIS SECTION. STOP THIS. STOP THIS, I SAY! THIS IS MY SHOW!

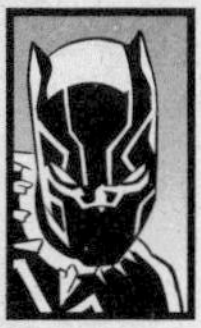

BLACK PANTHER: What a crybaby. His color scheme and web pattern are unnatural. I've never met a spider that looked and acted like this.

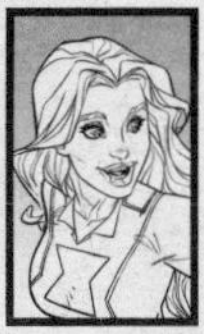

BLACK WIDOW: From one spider to another, this suit is a little too on the nose. Wait, do spiders have noses?

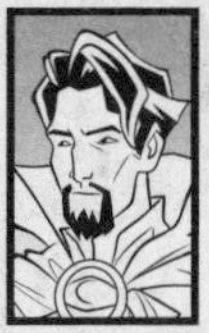

DOCTOR STRANGE: Spiders are naturally hairy. I would have liked to have seen a lot more hair. And fangs! Why don't I just turn him into a REAL spider?

WHEN YOU FINALLY KILL A GIANT SPIDER

AND IT EXPLODES INTO HUNDREDS OF BABY SPIDERS

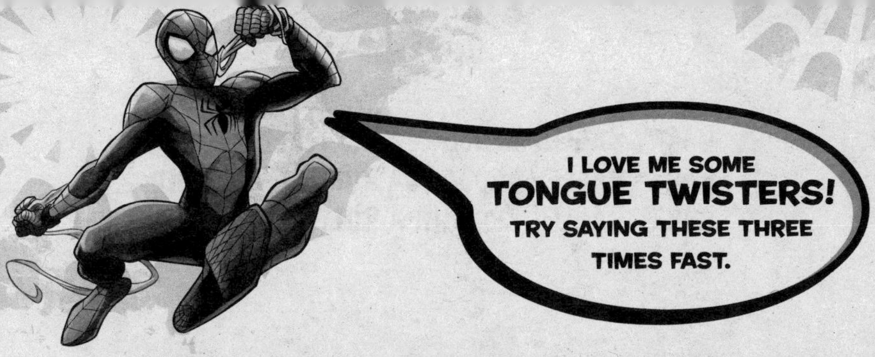
I LOVE ME SOME
TONGUE TWISTERS!
TRY SAYING THESE THREE
TIMES FAST.

A BIG BLACK BUG BIT A BIG BLACK BEAR.
A BIG BLACK BUG BIT A BIG BLACK BEAR.
A BIG BLACK BUG BIT A BIG BLACK BEAR.

RED LEATHER, YELLOW LEATHER.
RED LEATHER, YELLOW LEATHER.
RED LEATHER, YELLOW LEATHER.

PRETTY PINK PIGGY BANK.
PRETTY PINK PIGGY BANK.
PRETTY PINK PIGGY BANK.

SILLY SALLY SELLS SCENTED SHINGLES.
SILLY SALLY SELLS SCENTED SHINGLES.
SILLY SALLY SELLS SCENTED SHINGLES.

BARRY BAGLEY BROUGHT A BUTTERED BISCUIT.
BARRY BAGLEY BROUGHT A BUTTERED BISCUIT.
BARRY BAGLEY BROUGHT A BUTTERED BISCUIT.

PETER PARKER PICKED A PECK OF PICKLED PEPPERS.
HOW MANY PICKLED PEPPERS DID PETER PARKER PICK?
PETER PARKER PICKED A PECK OF PICKLED PEPPERS.
HOW MANY PICKLED PEPPERS DID PETER PARKER PICK?
PETER PARKER PICKED A PECK OF PICKLED PEPPERS.
HOW MANY PICKLED PEPPERS DID PETER PARKER PICK?

CRAZY CRISP CRUSTS CRACKLE AND CRUNCH.
CRAZY CRISP CRUSTS CRACKLE AND CRUNCH.
CRAZY CRISP CRUSTS CRACKLE AND CRUNCH.

THIS IS MAKING ME HUNGRY!

TONGUE TWISTERS

THE SKIMPY SKUNK SAT ON A STUMP AND THUNK THE
STUMP STUNK, BUT THE STUMP THUNK THE SKUNK STUNK.
THE SKIMPY SKUNK SAT ON A STUMP AND THUNK THE
STUMP STUNK, BUT THE STUMP THUNK THE SKUNK STUNK.
THE SKIMPY SKUNK SAT ON A STUMP AND THUNK THE
STUMP STUNK, BUT THE STUMP THUNK THE SKUNK STUNK.

 TANGY TACOS TAUNT TERRY'S TASTE BUDS.
TANGY TACOS TAUNT TERRY'S TASTE BUDS.
TANGY TACOS TAUNT TERRY'S TASTE BUDS.

 I THOUGHT A THOUGHT.
BUT THE THOUGHT I THOUGHT WASN'T THE THOUGHT
I THOUGHT I THOUGHT.

PETER PARKER ALWAYS SEEMS TO DISAPPEAR WHEN SPIDER-MAN SHOWS UP.
BUT . . . THAT'S NONE OF MY BUSINESS.

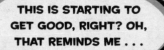

THIS IS STARTING TO GET GOOD, RIGHT? OH, THAT REMINDS ME . . .

WHAT DID THE HOT DOG SAY WHEN HE WON THE RACE?

I'M A **WIENER!**

OKAY, NOW I'M HUNGRY **AGAIN.**

NOW IT'S TIME TO TAKE THINGS TO THE **NEXT LEVEL.** TURN THE PAGE. **OR ARE YOU AFRAID?!** (DON'T BE.)

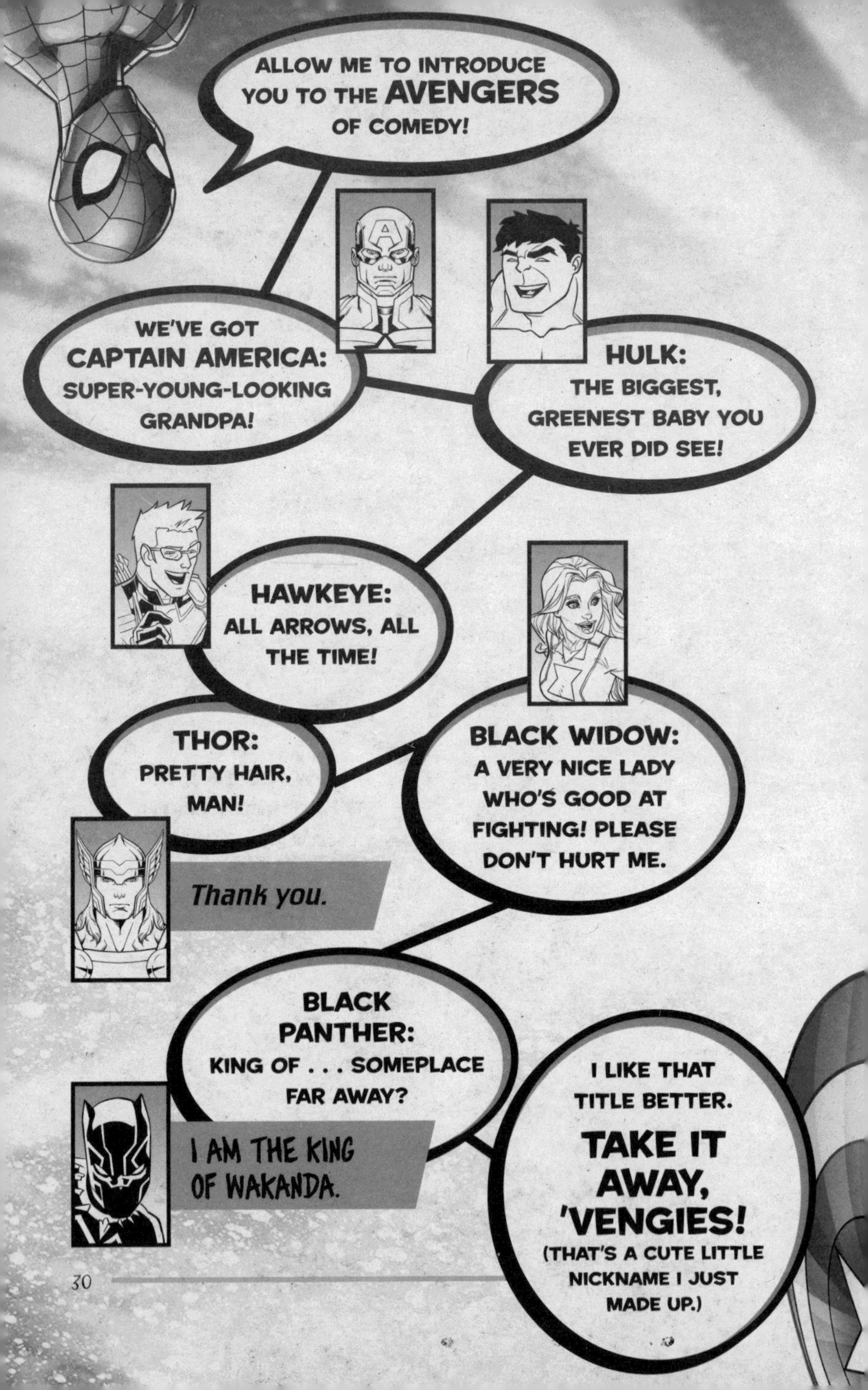
ALLOW ME TO INTRODUCE YOU TO THE AVENGERS OF COMEDY!
WE'VE GOT CAPTAIN AMERICA: SUPER-YOUNG-LOOKING GRANDPA!
HULK: THE BIGGEST, GREENEST BABY YOU EVER DID SEE!
HAWKEYE: ALL ARROWS, ALL THE TIME!
THOR: PRETTY HAIR, MAN!
Thank you.
BLACK WIDOW: A VERY NICE LADY WHO'S GOOD AT FIGHTING! PLEASE DON'T HURT ME.
BLACK PANTHER: KING OF . . . SOMEPLACE FAR AWAY?
I AM THE KING OF WAKANDA.
I LIKE THAT TITLE BETTER. TAKE IT AWAY, 'VENGIES! (THAT'S A CUTE LITTLE NICKNAME I JUST MADE UP.)

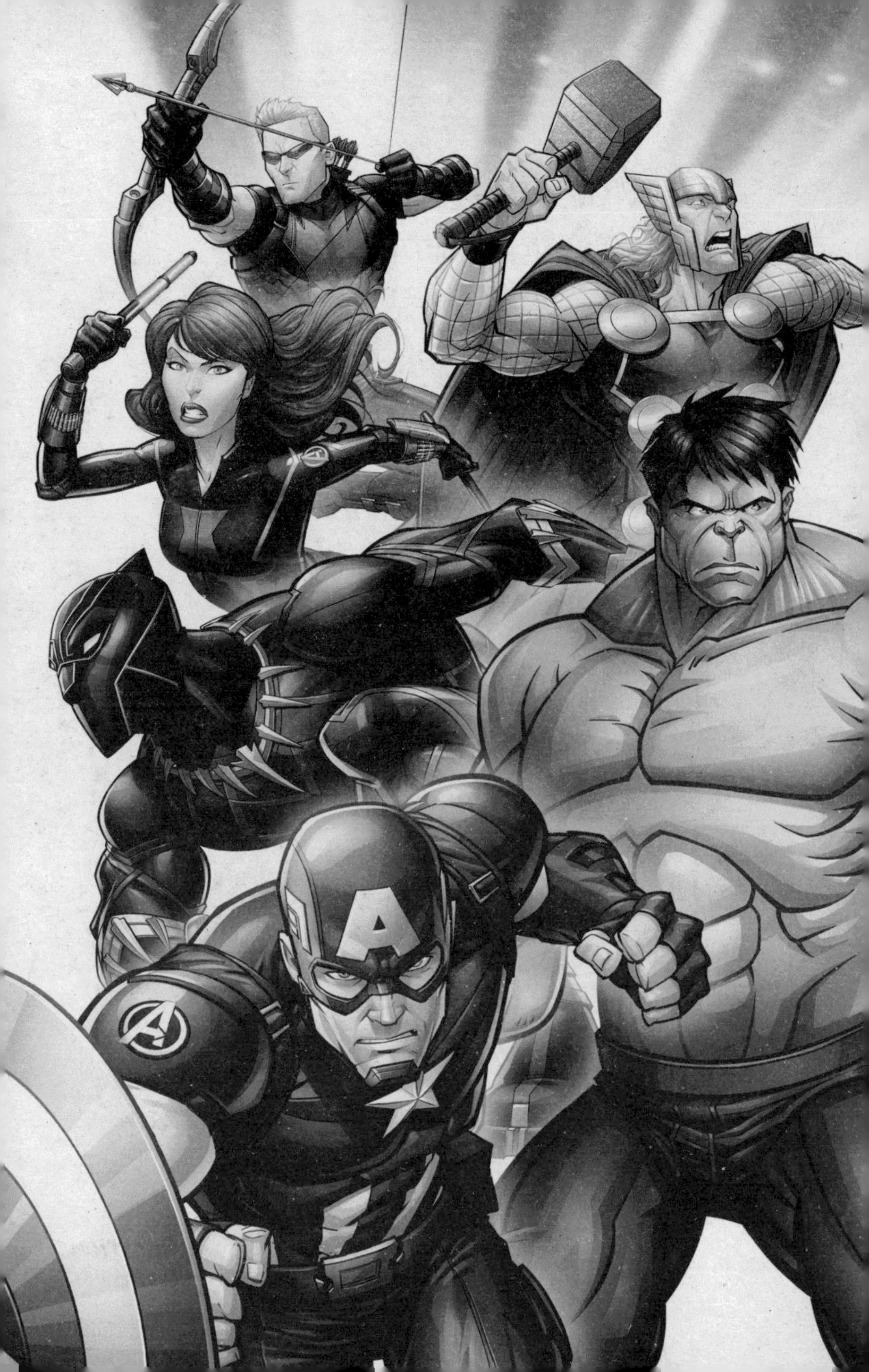

???

Q: What's Thor's favorite food?

A: **Thor-tillas.**

*'Tis true! I, son of Odin, do **enjoy** a yummy snack.*

???

Q: What do you call Iron Man without his suit?

A: **Stark naked!**

???

Q: When do ducks wake up?

A: **The quack of dawn.**

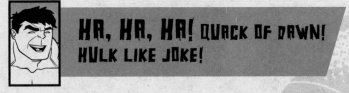

HA, HA, HA! QUACK OF DAWN! HULK LIKE JOKE!

???

Q: Why should you eat a cupcake in the rain?

A: **You'll get more sprinkles!**

??? Questions
& Answers

???

Q: What did Iron Man win for coming in first place?
A: A gold metal!

True. Remember, I'm good at EVERYTHING.

???

Q: Why did the orange stop in the middle of the road?
A: It ran out of juice!

???

Q: What did Thor become after he wrote a book?
A: An auTHOR.

???

Q: What do you give Hulk when he's feeling sick?
A: Plenty of room!

HULK NO LIKE THAT JOKE.

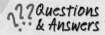

Questions & Answers

Q: What's Black Panther's favorite day of the week?

A: Cat-urday.

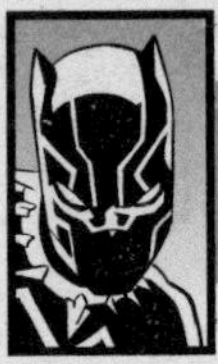

I'M NOT AN **ACTUAL** CAT. YOU KNOW THAT, RIGHT?

Q: Why is Iron Man like a Russian nesting doll?

A: Because he's full of himself.

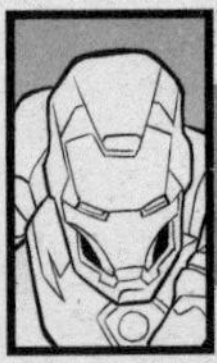

HEY! That's not totally true! (But I do look amazing underneath all this armor.)

Q: What do you call a guy that looks like Thor's brother?

A: A Loki-like.

Q: What did the police do when the evil barber escaped from prison?
A: They combed the area.

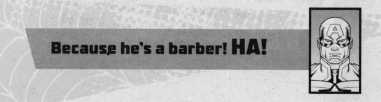

Because he's a barber! HA!

Q: What's Hulk's favorite side dish?
A: Smashed potatoes.

Q: What did the archer wear to a formal event?
A: A bow tie!

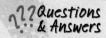

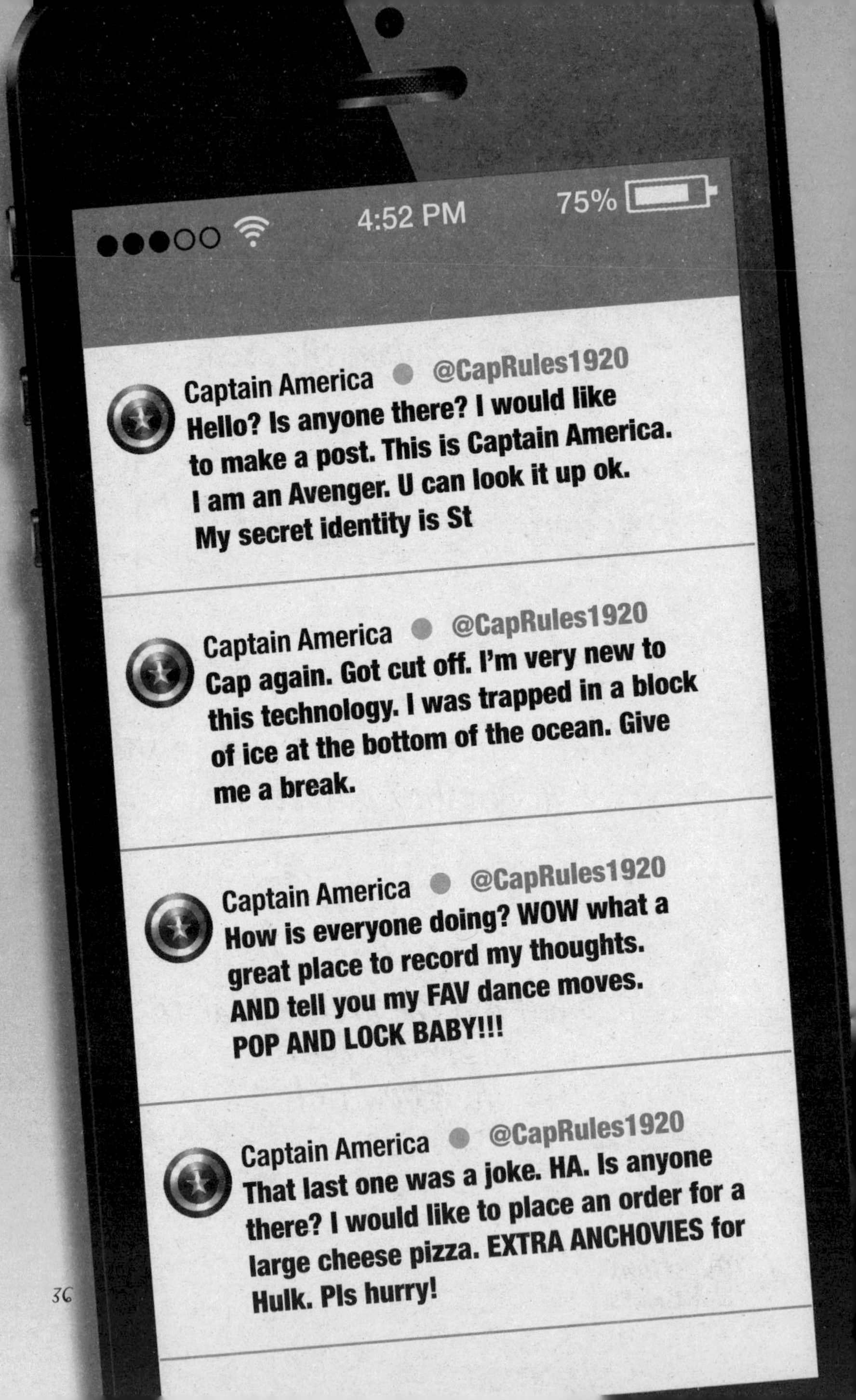
●●●○○
4:52 PM
75%
Captain America @CapRules1920
Hello? Is anyone there? I would like
to make a post. This is Captain America.
I am an Avenger. U can look it up ok.
My secret identity is St
Captain America @CapRules1920
Cap again. Got cut off. I'm very new to
this technology. I was trapped in a block
of ice at the bottom of the ocean. Give
me a break.
Captain America @CapRules1920
How is everyone doing? WOW what a
great place to record my thoughts.
AND tell you my FAV dance moves.
POP AND LOCK BABY!!!
Captain America @CapRules1920
That last one was a joke. HA. Is anyone
there? I would like to place an order for a
large cheese pizza. EXTRA ANCHOVIES for
Hulk. Pls hurry!

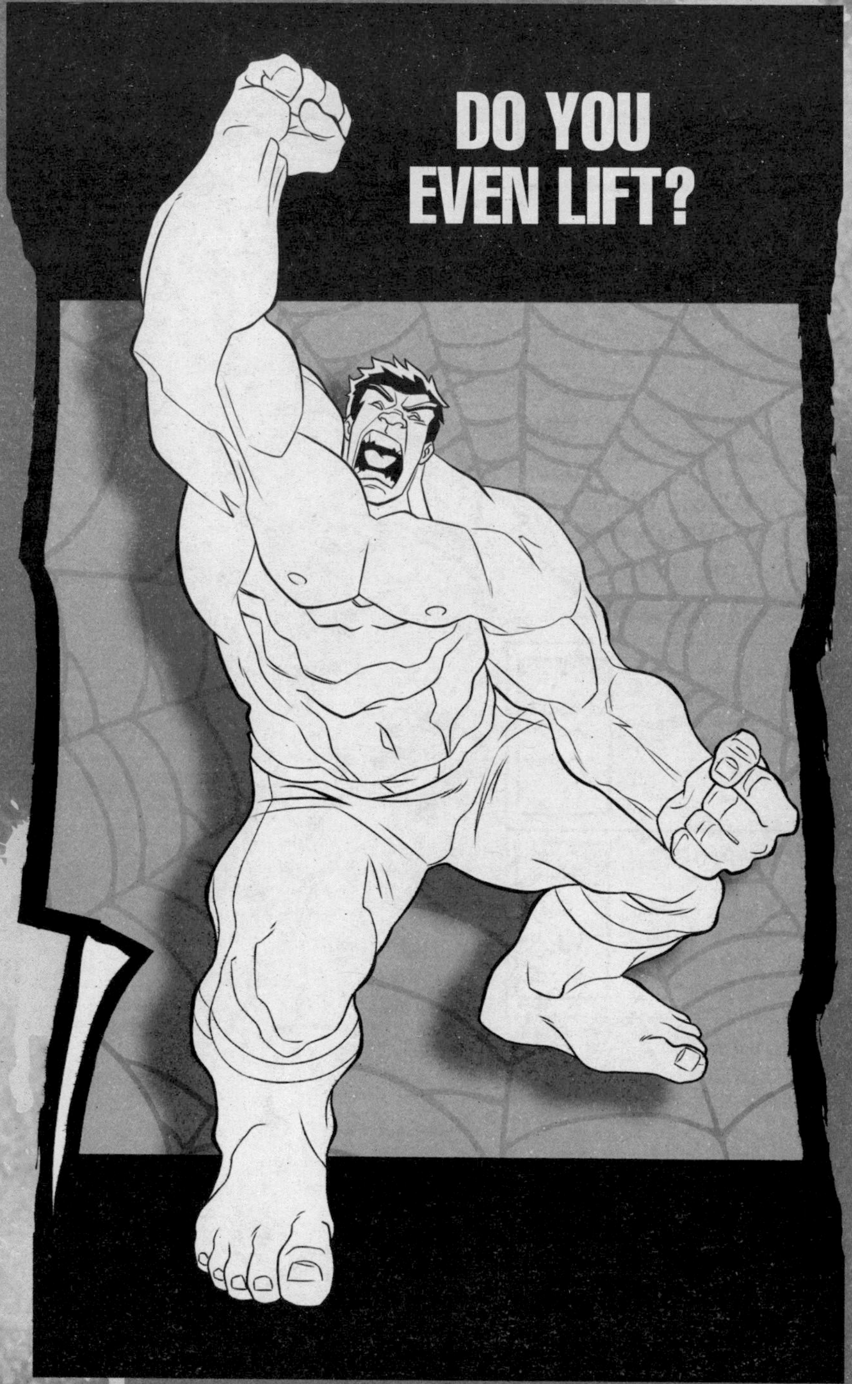
DO YOU
EVEN LIFT?

COSTUME PATROL

DAGGER? DRAG HER!

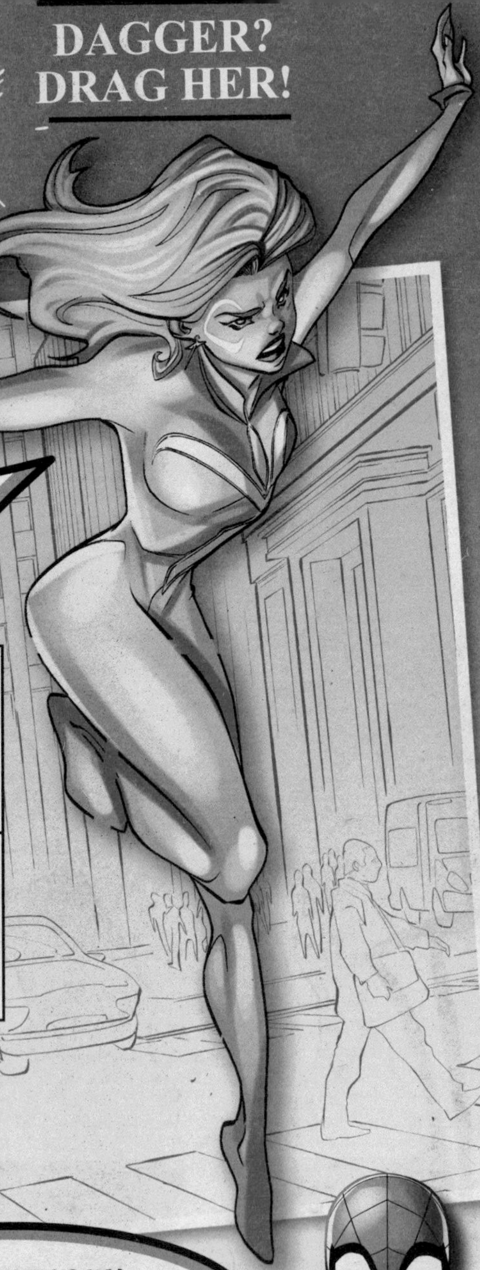
Hey! Whoa. What is this? What's the Costume Patrol?

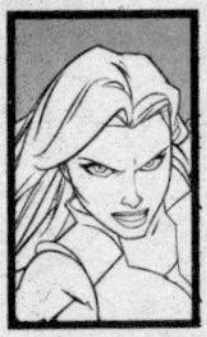

GAMORA: We are the costume patrol. You are in violation of our code. Garments of this color will NOT be worn after Labor Day.

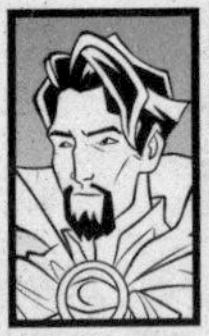

DOCTOR STRANGE: Meh. Not a fan of the bodysuit. Personally, I prefer a big, flowing cape. And where are the fun accessories? She needs more jewelry. LOTS of jewelry.

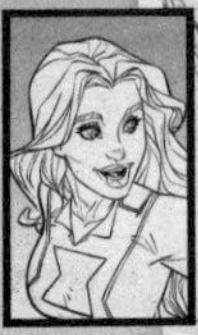

BLACK WIDOW: Watch it, Strange. Bodysuits allow a fighter to move effortlessly when dealing with an attacking opponent. Plus, they're SO easy to clean.

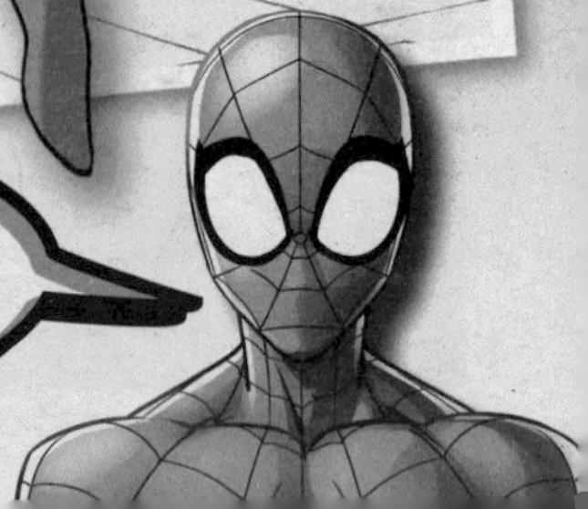
EASY TO CLEAN? HA!
ONE SPILL OF MY FRUIT PUNCH AND IT'S OVER. MMMM. NOW I'M THIRSTY. FOR FASHION. OKURRRR!

Knock, knock.
Who's there?
Thor.
Thor who?
Thor-y about some of
these jokes.

Knock, knock.
Who's there?
Atch.
Atch who?
Bless you!

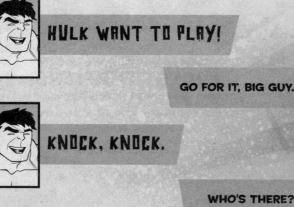

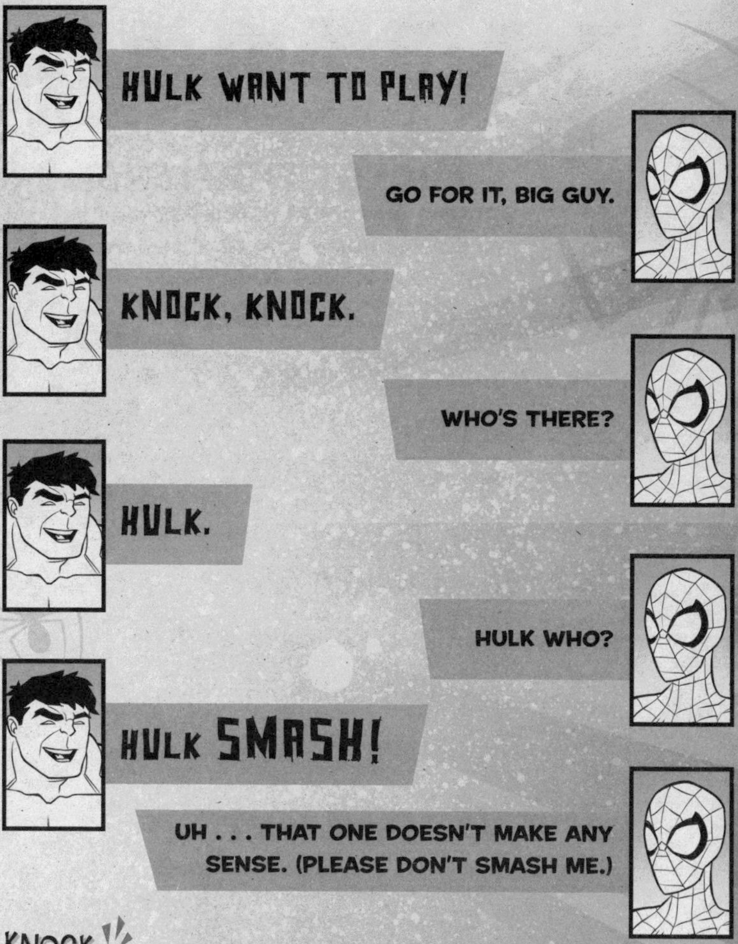

HULK WANT TO PLAY!

GO FOR IT, BIG GUY.

KNOCK, KNOCK.

WHO'S THERE?

HULK.

HULK WHO?

HULK SMASH!

UH . . . THAT ONE DOESN'T MAKE ANY
SENSE. (PLEASE DON'T SMASH ME.)

KNOCK-
KNOCK

Spidey's OPEN MIC SPOTLIGHT:

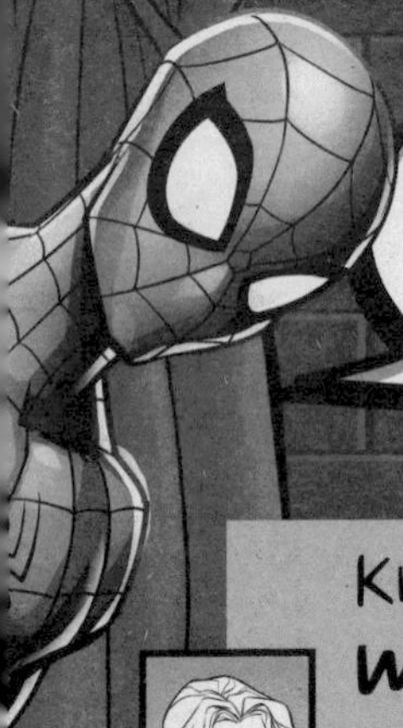

COMING TO THE STAGE RIGHT NOW IS ONE OF THE **FIERCEST FIGHTERS** AROUND AND AN AMAZING AVENGER TO BOOT. LADIES AND GENTLEMAN, PUT YOUR HANDS TOGETHER FOR **BLACK WIDOW!**

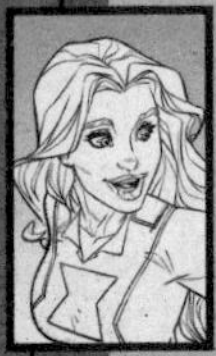

Knock, knock.
Who's there?
A broken pencil.
A broken pencil who?
Never mind.
It's pointless.

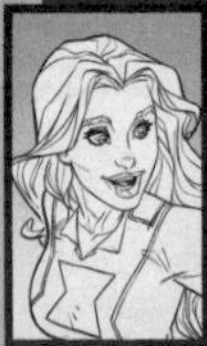

Q: What do you get when you mix a toad with the sun?
A: Star warts.

Black Widow

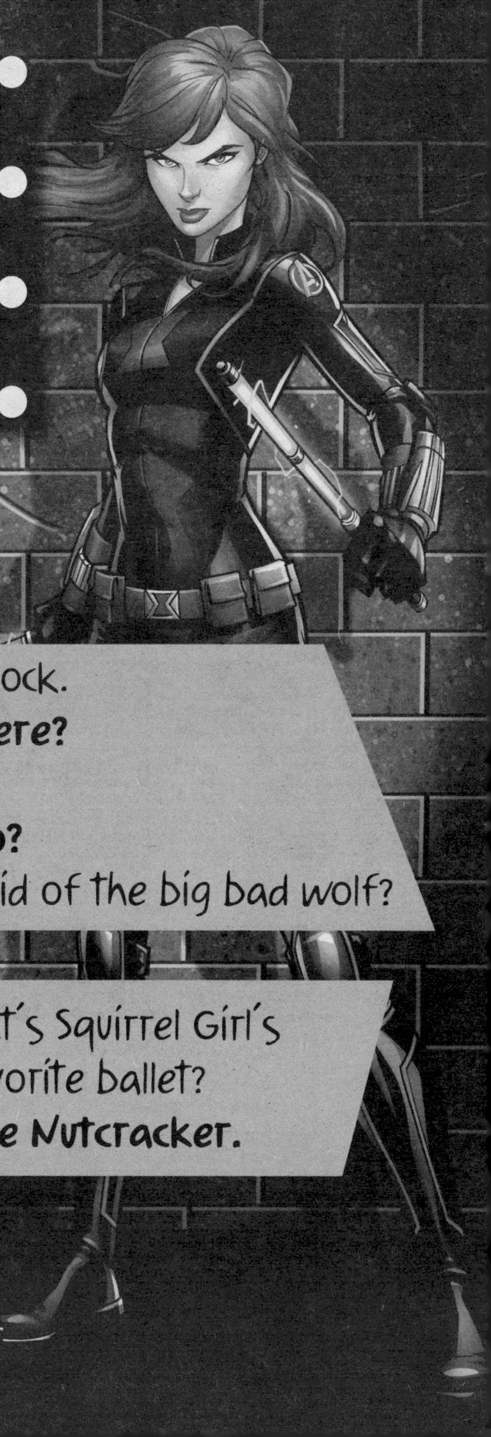

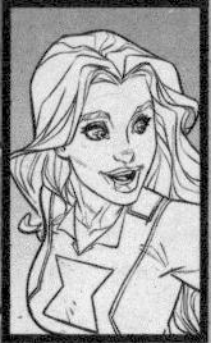

Knock, knock.

Who's there?

Ooze.

Ooze who?

Ooze afraid of the big bad wolf?

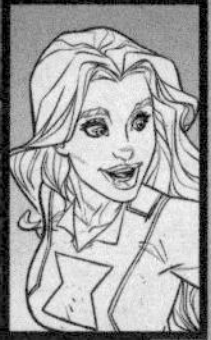

Q: What's Squirrel Girl's favorite ballet?

A: The Nutcracker.

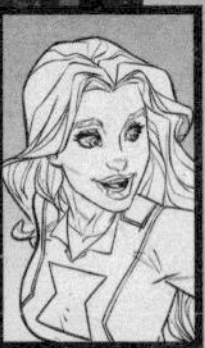

Q: What do you call an elephant that wears perfume?

A: A smell-e-phant.

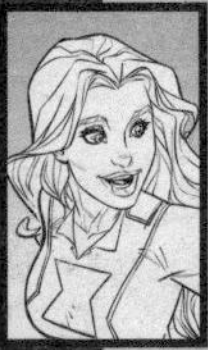

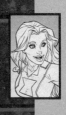

Knock, knock.

Who's there?

Spell.

Spell who?

W-H-O.

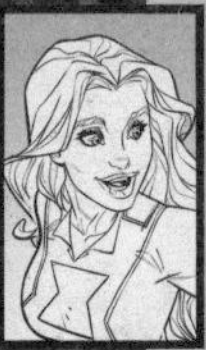

Q: What do you call a fake noodle?

A: An impasta.

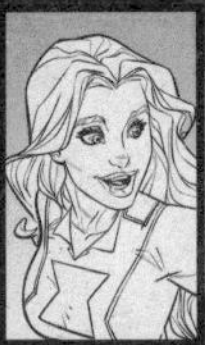

Sometimes black widow spiders can kill their mates.

UM, THAT'S **NOT** A JOKE. THAT'S JUST A FACT.

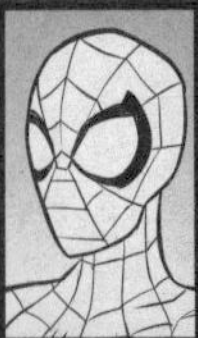

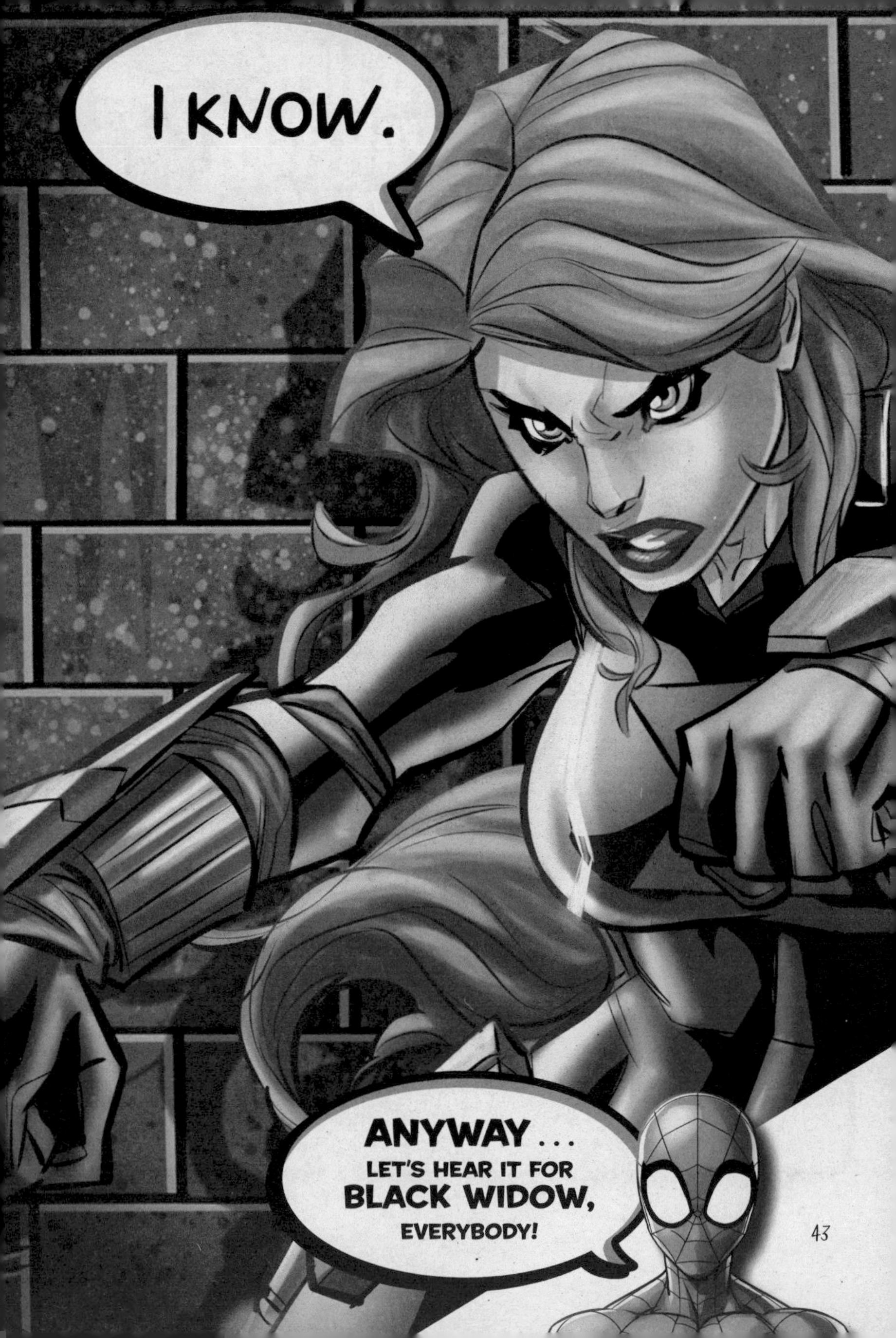
I KNOW.
ANYWAY . . . LET'S HEAR IT FOR BLACK WIDOW, EVERYBODY!

WHEN THE TEACHER SAYS FIND A PARTNER, AND YOU AND YOUR BFF LOCK EYES FROM ACROSS THE ROOM.

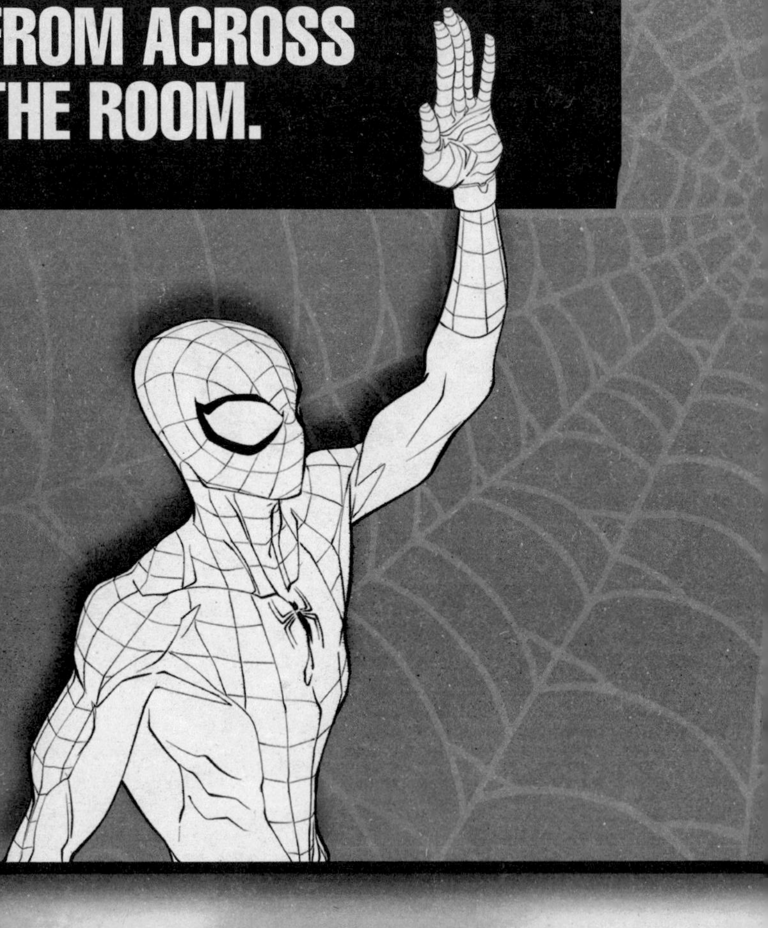

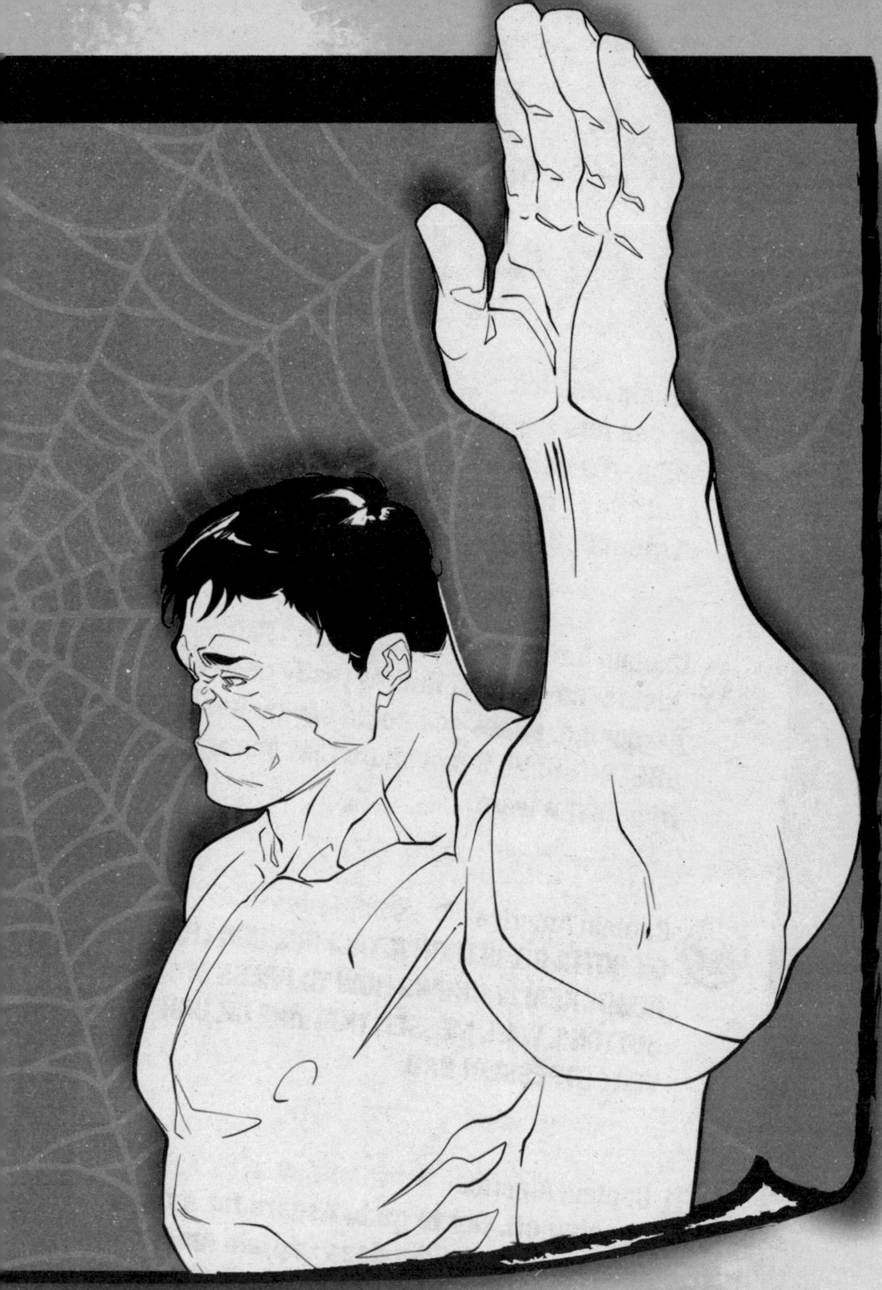

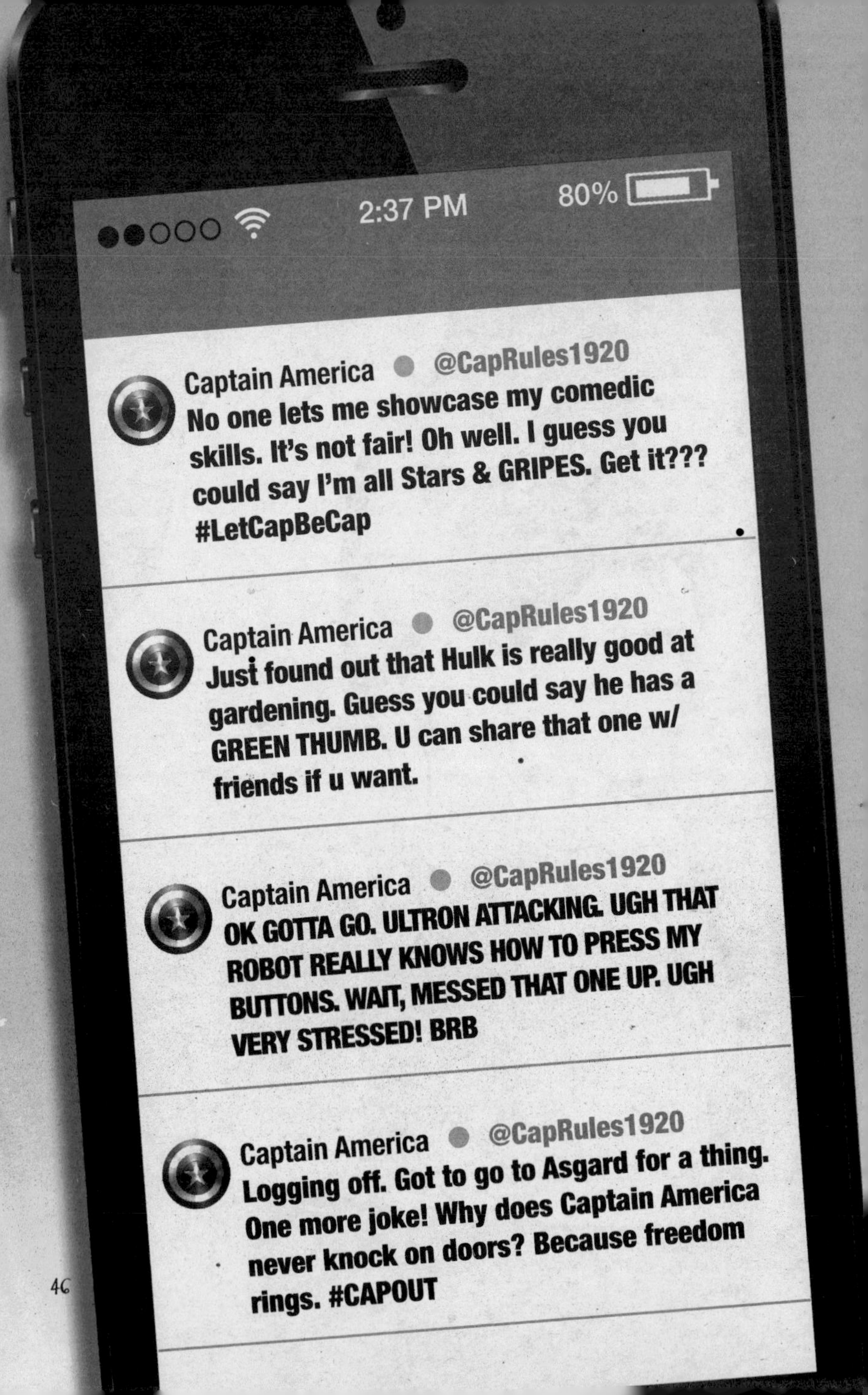
●●○○○
2:37 PM
80%
Captain America ● @CapRules1920
No one lets me showcase my comedic
skills. It's not fair! Oh well. I guess you
could say I'm all Stars & GRIPES. Get it???
#LetCapBeCap
Captain America ● @CapRules1920
Just found out that Hulk is really good at
gardening. Guess you could say he has a
GREEN THUMB. U can share that one w/
friends if u want.
Captain America ● @CapRules1920
OK GOTTA GO. ULTRON ATTACKING. UGH THAT
ROBOT REALLY KNOWS HOW TO PRESS MY
BUTTONS. WAIT, MESSED THAT ONE UP. UGH
VERY STRESSED! BRB
Captain America ● @CapRules1920
Logging off. Got to go to Asgard for a thing.
One more joke! Why does Captain America
never knock on doors? Because freedom
rings. #CAPOUT

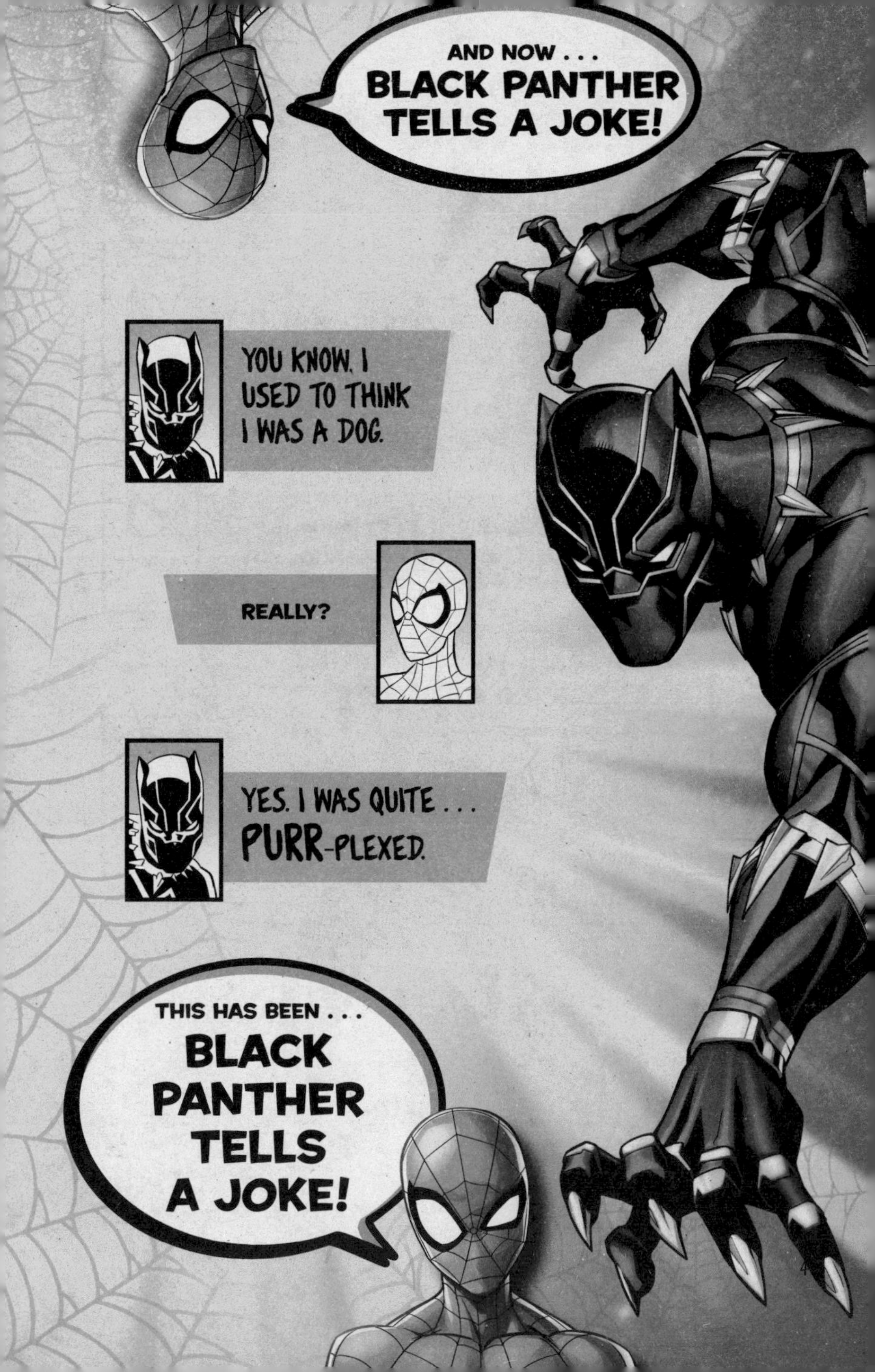
AND NOW . . .
BLACK PANTHER TELLS A JOKE!
YOU KNOW, I USED TO THINK I WAS A DOG.
REALLY?
YES. I WAS QUITE . . . PURR-PLEXED.
THIS HAS BEEN . . .
BLACK PANTHER TELLS A JOKE!

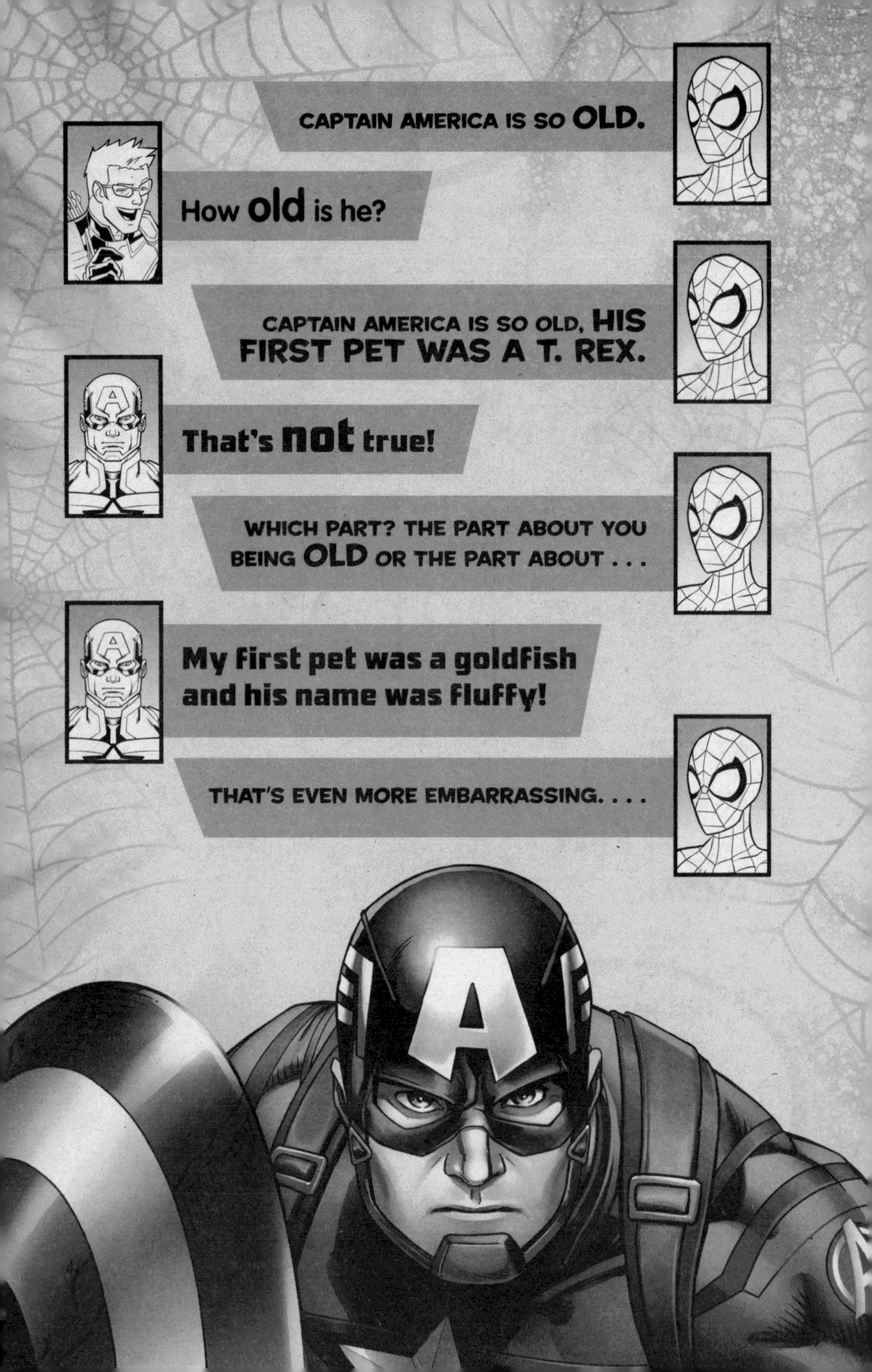
CAPTAIN AMERICA IS SO OLD.
How old is he?
CAPTAIN AMERICA IS SO OLD, HIS FIRST PET WAS A T. REX.
That's not true!
WHICH PART? THE PART ABOUT YOU BEING OLD OR THE PART ABOUT . . .
My first pet was a goldfish and his name was Fluffy!
THAT'S EVEN MORE EMBARRASSING. . . .

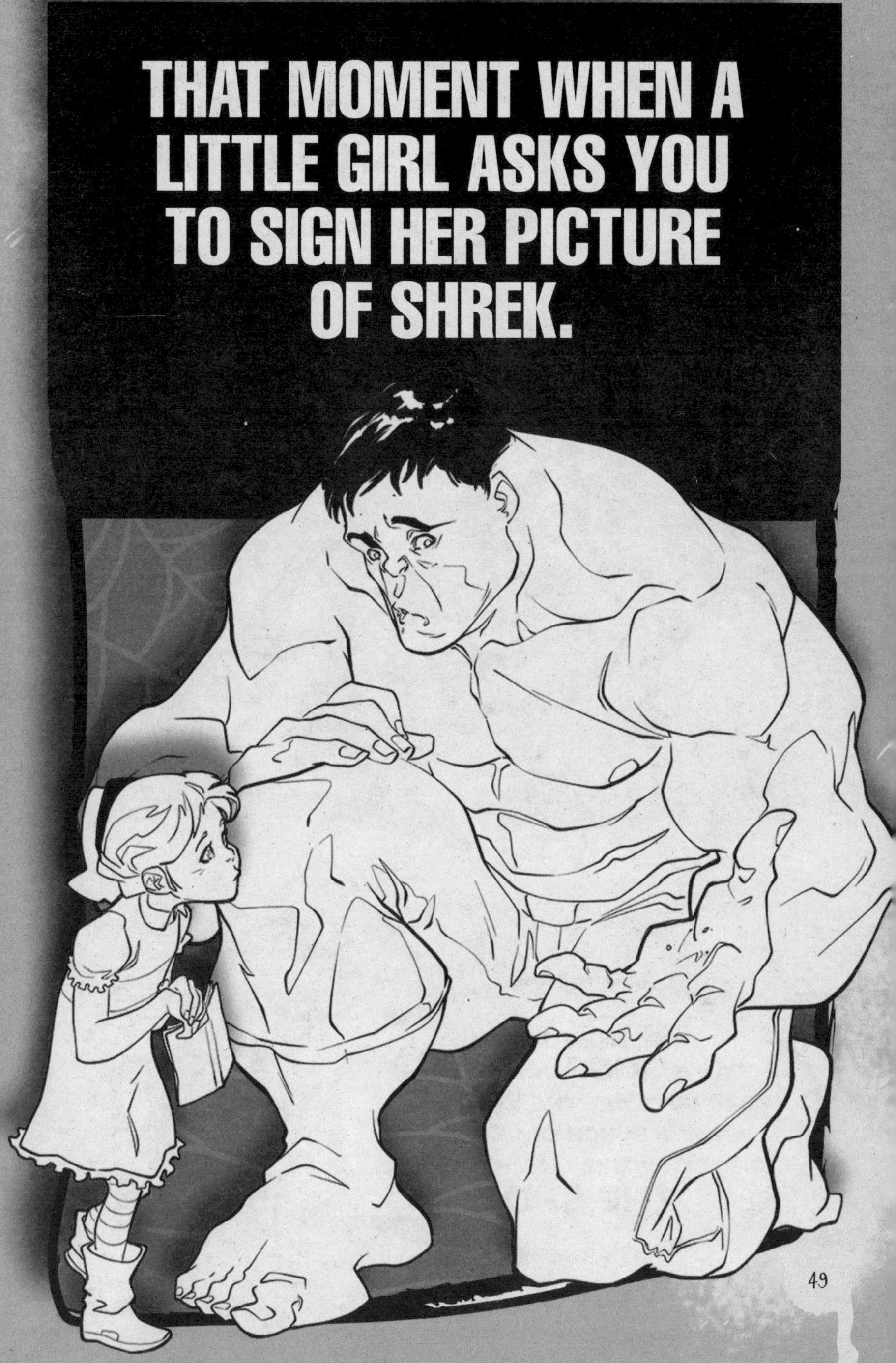
THAT MOMENT WHEN A LITTLE GIRL ASKS YOU TO SIGN HER PICTURE OF SHREK.

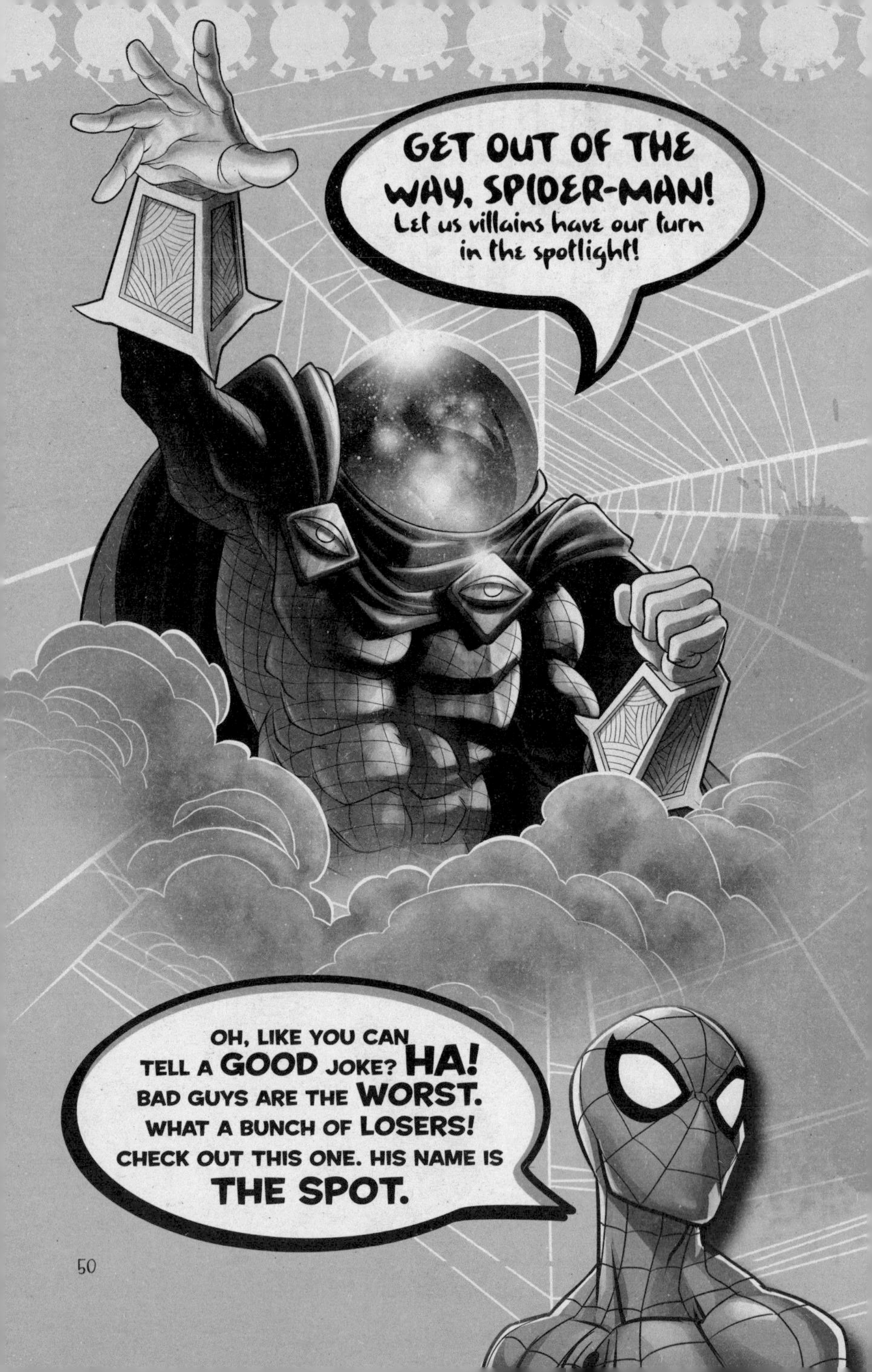
GET OUT OF THE WAY, SPIDER-MAN! Let us villains have our turn in the spotlight!
OH, LIKE YOU CAN TELL A GOOD JOKE? HA! BAD GUYS ARE THE WORST. WHAT A BUNCH OF LOSERS! CHECK OUT THIS ONE. HIS NAME IS THE SPOT.

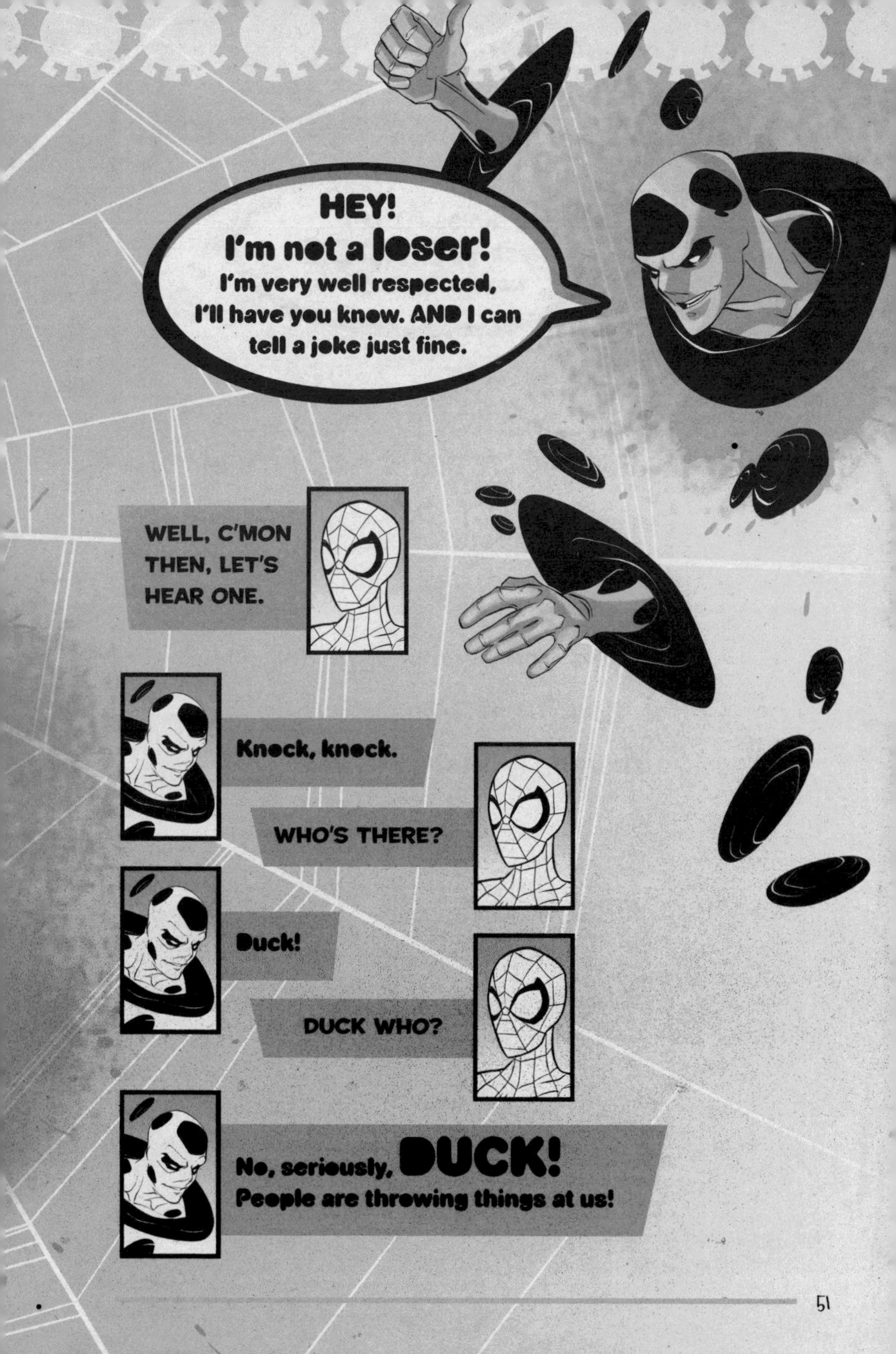
HEY!
I'm not a loser!
I'm very well respected, I'll have you know. AND I can tell a joke just fine.
WELL, C'MON THEN, LET'S HEAR ONE.
Knock, knock.
WHO'S THERE?
Duck!
DUCK WHO?
No, seriously, DUCK!
People are throwing things at us!

I GUESS I'LL LET THESE **WEIRDOS** HAVE A CHANCE.

???

Q: What's Doctor Octopus's favorite month?
A: October.

???

Q: Did you hear about the
zombie hairdresser?
A: She dyed on the job.

???

Q: Where does Morbius the Living Vampire
store his money?
A: In a blood bank.

???

Q: Where does a bee sit?
A: On its bee-hind.

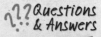

??? Questions
& Answers

???

Q: Why is the Lizard so good at creeping up on people?
A: Because he's a crept-tile.

???

Q: What kinds of fish don't swim?
A: Dead ones.

THAT'S **HARSH.**

We're villains. what did you **expect?**

???

Q: What do you call the Rhino in a phone booth?
A: Stuck!

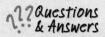

??

Q: How did the Vulture learn to fly?
A: **He winged it.**

??

Q: What crime did Doctor Octopus
commit at the bank?
A: **Armed robbery.**

??

Q: Why is Norman Osborn such
a messy eater?
A: **Because he's always Goblin.**

CLEVER!

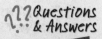

??Questions
& Answers

WHEN YOU GET AN INVITE FROM SOMEONE YOU HATE, BUT YOU KNOW YOU'RE GOING TO GO ANYWAY JUST TO RUIN IT FOR EVERYONE

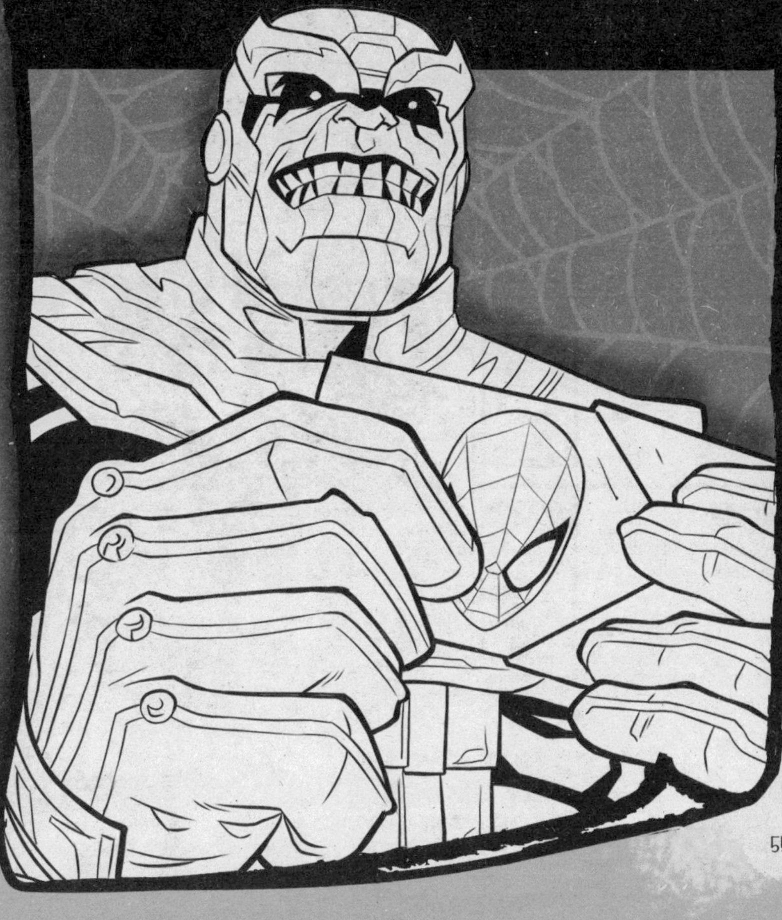

COSTUME PATROL

GUILTY AS CHARGED!

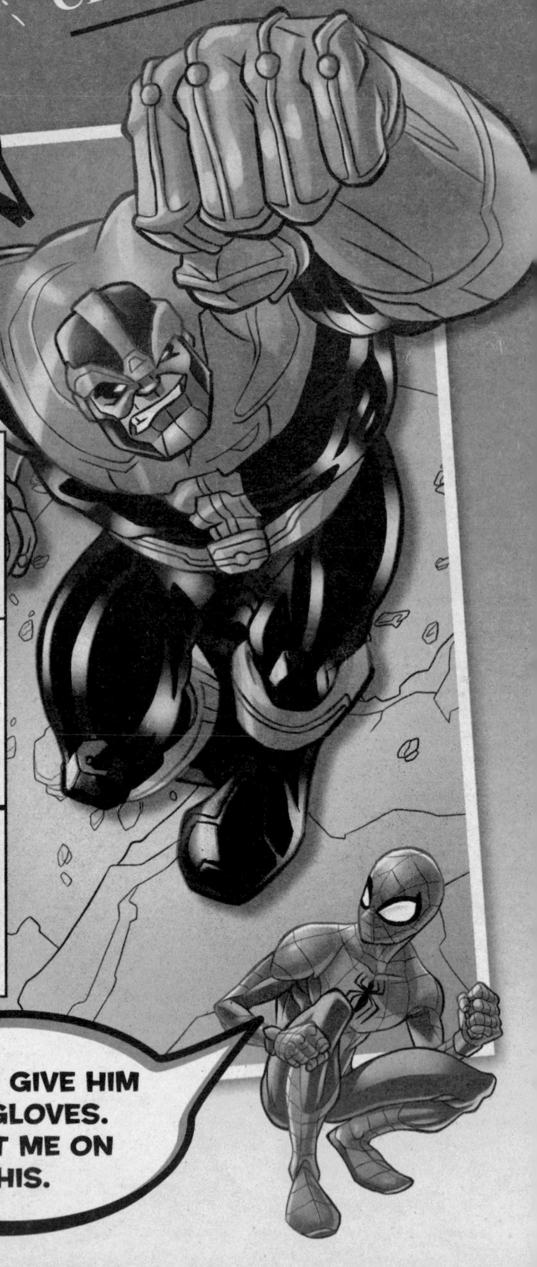
I will NOT be judged by the likes of YOU!
DO NOT GIVE HIM ANY GLOVES. TRUST ME ON THIS.

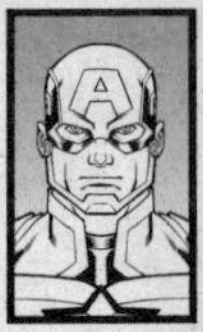

CAPTAIN AMERICA: Thanos's outfit is a true crime of fashion. He should be jailed for his poor layering skills.

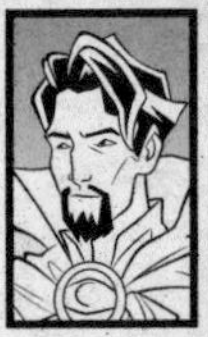

DOCTOR STRANGE: The chunky metal helmet isn't doing him any favors. What's he hiding under there? And why is he so angry?

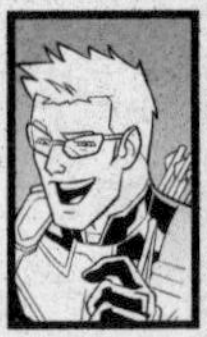

HAWKEYE: He needs an accessory. Like a glove with a bunch of bright, colorful stones on it. Something that says "I'm in control of this universe, and I like it."

Q: What was the Tyrannosaurus rex's diagnosis?
A: He had a dino-sore throat.

Q: Why did the boy bring a skunk to school?
A: For show-and-smell.

???

Q: How do you make a spider float?
A: Throw it in a root beer and add two scoops of vanilla ice cream.

???

Q: What kind of pants do ghosts wear?
A: Boo jeans.

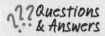

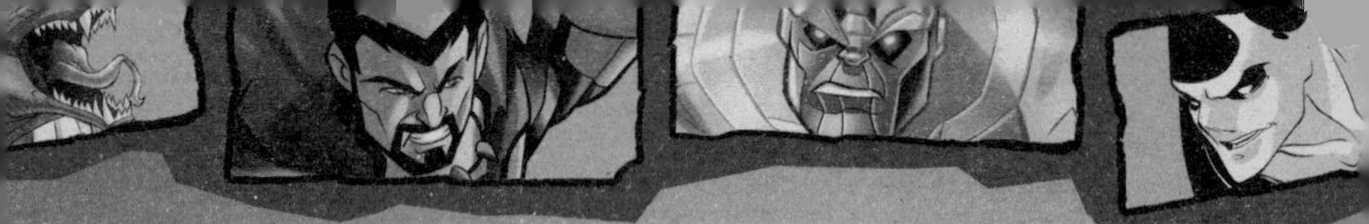

Q: Why couldn't the snake talk?
A: **He had a frog in his throat.**

Q: What do pigs eat when it's freezing outside?
A: **Slop sickles.**

Q: How did Doctor Octopus prepare to battle Spider-Man?
A: **He made sure he was well armed.**

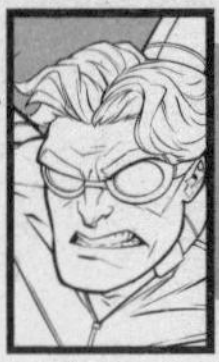

Maybe if I get MORE arms, I'll finally be able to **defeat Spider-Man!**

Q: When is a booger not a booger?
   A: When it's snot.

Q: What kind of dog does Dracula own?
   A: A bloodhound.

Q: Where is the best place to talk to a giant
   slimy monster?
   A: From far away!

Q: What's a sea monster's
   favorite sandwich?
   A: A sub!

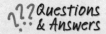

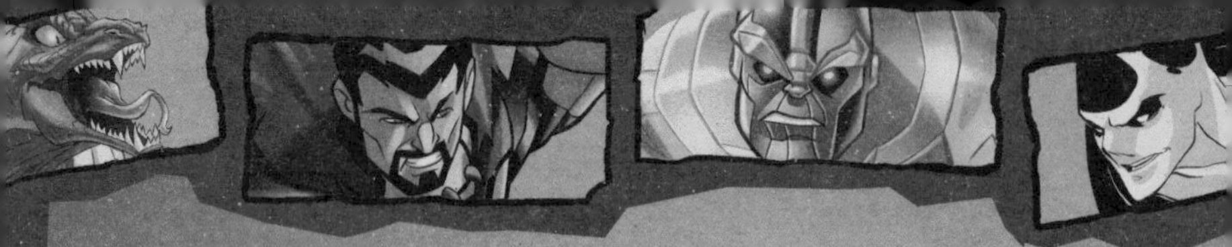

Q: What did the zombie order at the restaurant?

A: The waiter.

Q: What do sea monsters eat?

A: Fish and ships.

Q: What do you call a lizard who likes hip-hop?

A: A rap-tile!

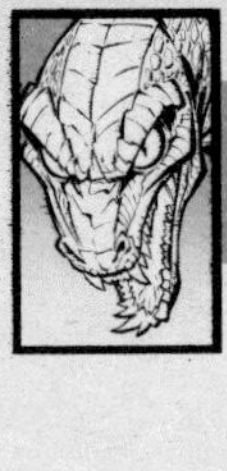

Sssseriously ssssick, sssson.

COSTUME PATROL

THE HUNT FOR FASHION

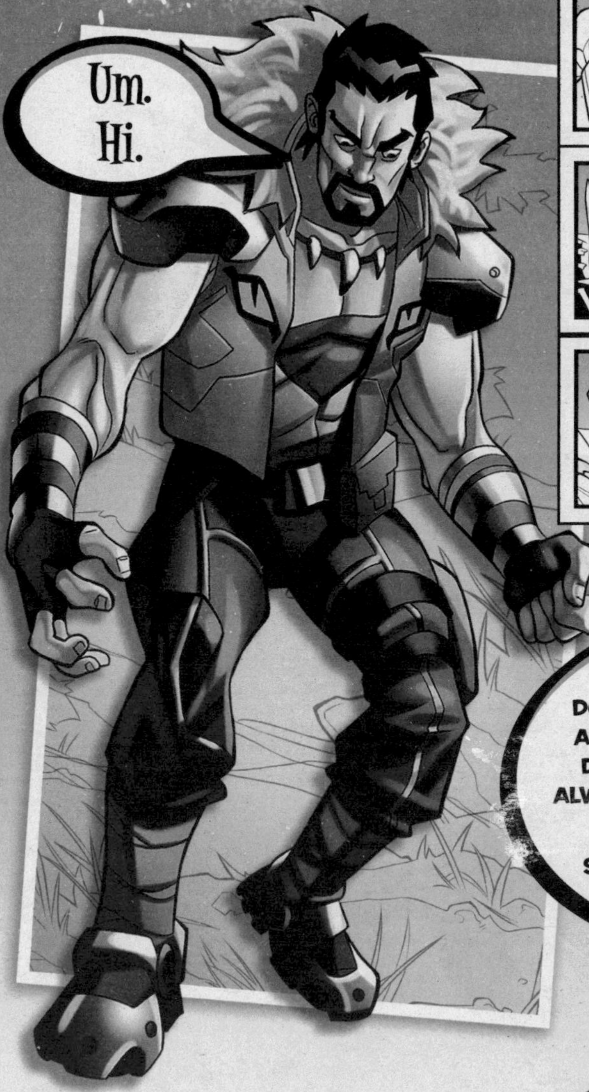
Um.
Hi.

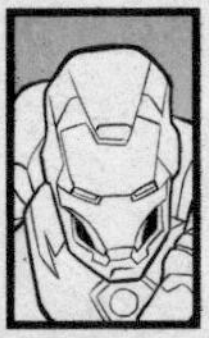

IRON MAN: UGH. Where do I begin? This is what happens when you let lions and tigers give you advice on your outfit.

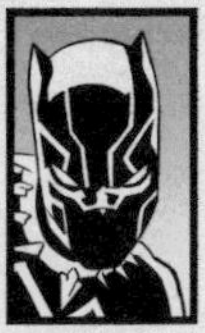

BLACK PANTHER: Men who stalk beasts for their hides are WEAK. I will show this one who is the hunter and who is the prey.

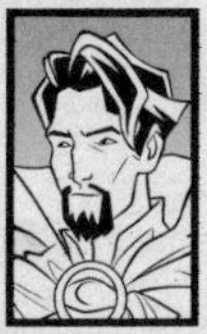

DOCTOR STRANGE: His mane looks so fluffy and fun! I wish I had a fluffy mane on my costume. Call me DOCTOR FLUFF.

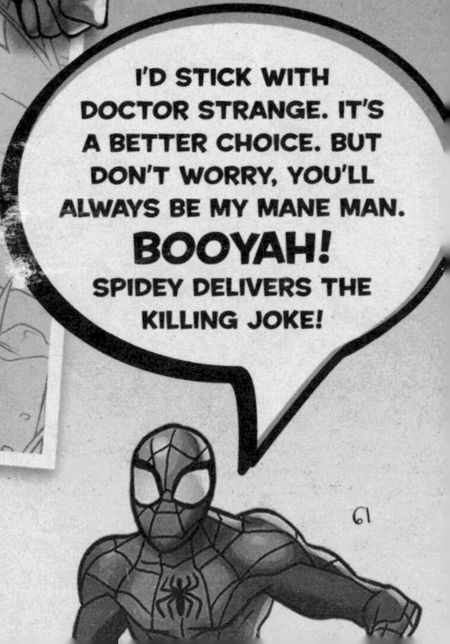
I'D STICK WITH DOCTOR STRANGE. IT'S A BETTER CHOICE. BUT DON'T WORRY, YOU'LL ALWAYS BE MY MANE MAN.
BOOYAH!
SPIDEY DELIVERS THE KILLING JOKE!

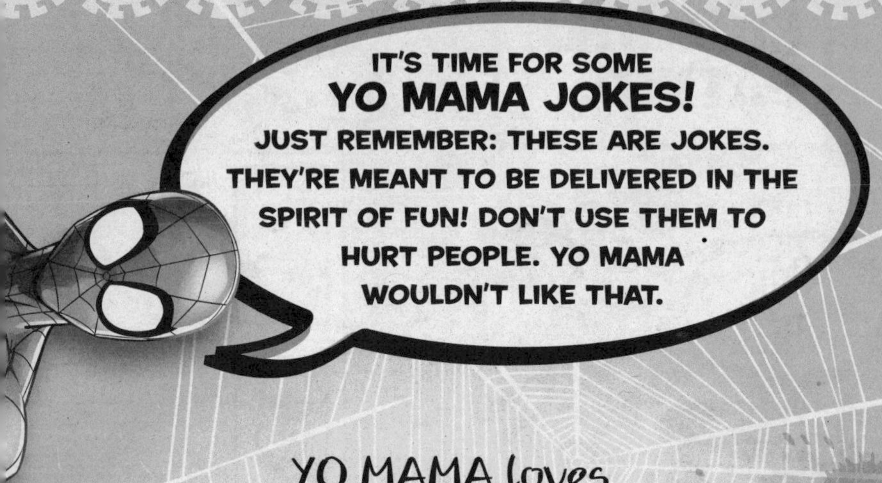
IT'S TIME FOR SOME YO MAMA JOKES! JUST REMEMBER: THESE ARE JOKES. THEY'RE MEANT TO BE DELIVERED IN THE SPIRIT OF FUN! DON'T USE THEM TO HURT PEOPLE. YO MAMA WOULDN'T LIKE THAT.

YO MAMA loves
ice cream so much,
her blood type is chocolate chip!

YO MAMA's so old,
she took her driver's test
on a dinosaur!

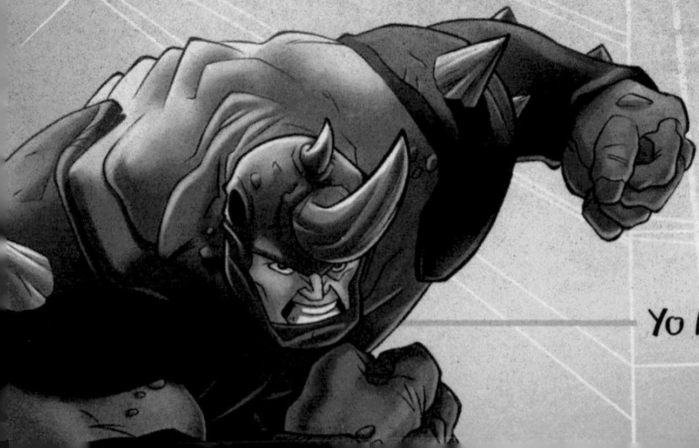

YO MAMA is so short, she uses a sock for a sleeping bag!

YO MAMA's breath is so bad, when she yawns, her teeth duck!

YO MAMA is so chatty, the only place she's ever invited is outside!

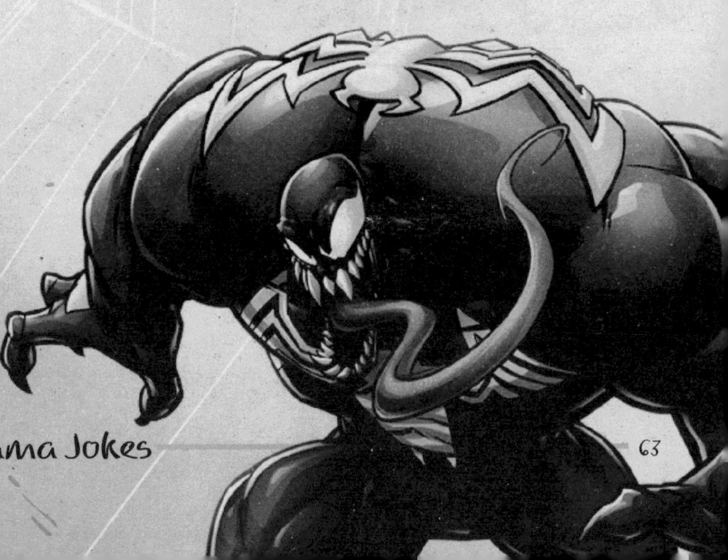

YO MAMA is so mean that Doc Ock
doesn't even like her!

YO MAMA is so old,
when she was born the Dead Sea
was just getting sick!

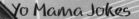
Yo Mama Jokes

YO MAMA is so weird,
I caught her yelling into the
mailbox and when I asked her
what she was doing she said,
"Sending a voice mail."

YO MAMA is so silly,
I asked her to speak her mind and
she stayed silent!

YO MAMA is so weird,
she entered a weirdo contest and
they said, "Sorry, we don't allow
professionals!"

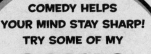

COMEDY HELPS
YOUR MIND STAY SHARP!
TRY SOME OF MY
RIDDLES
ON FOR SIZE. ARE YOU
SMARTER THAN THESE
DOOFUSES?

Q: What has a face and two hands
   but no arms or legs?
A: A clock!

Q: What goes up and doesn't come
   back down?
A: Your age.

Q: What travels around the world
   but stays in one spot?
A: A stamp!

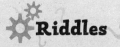

Riddles

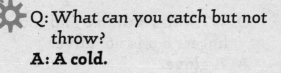

Q: What can you catch but not throw?

A: A cold.

Q: What occurs once in a minute, twice in a moment, and never in one thousand years?

A: The letter M.

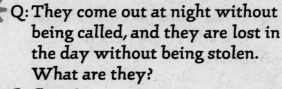

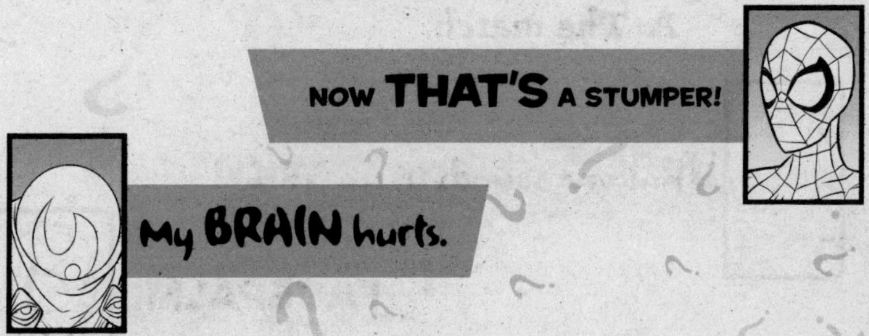

NOW **THAT'S** A STUMPER!

My **BRAIN** hurts.

Q: They come out at night without being called, and they are lost in the day without being stolen. What are they?

A: Stars!

Q: Which weighs more, a pound of feathers or a pound of bricks?

A: Neither, they both weigh one pound!

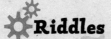**Riddles** ————————————

Q: What has a thumb and four
   fingers but is not alive?
A: **A glove.**

Q: You walk into a room with
   a match, a kerosene lamp, a
   candle, and a fireplace.
   Which do you light first?
A: **The match.**

That one sounds like a TRICK!

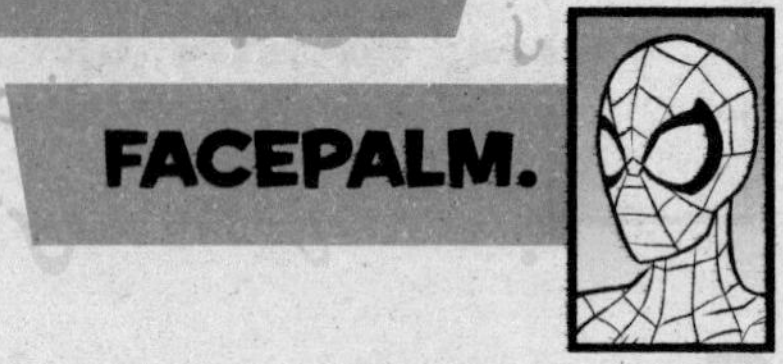

FACEPALM.

Q: What word becomes shorter when
   you add two letters to it?
A: **Short.**

Q: If a blue house is made of blue bricks,
   a yellow house is made of yellow
   bricks, and a red house is made of red
   bricks, what is a greenhouse made of?
A: **Glass.**

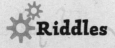 **Riddles**

Q: What has a neck but no head?
A: A bottle.

Q: What is at the end of a rainbow?

 A pot of GOLD!

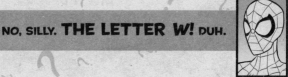 NO, SILLY. **THE LETTER W!** DUH.

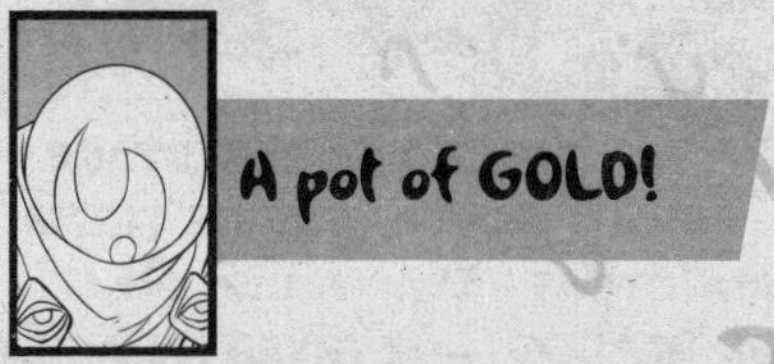

Q: Take away my first letter, and I still sound the same. Take away my last letter, I still sound the same. Even take away my letter in the middle, I will still sound the same. I'm a five-letter word. What am I?
A: Empty.

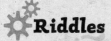 **Riddles**

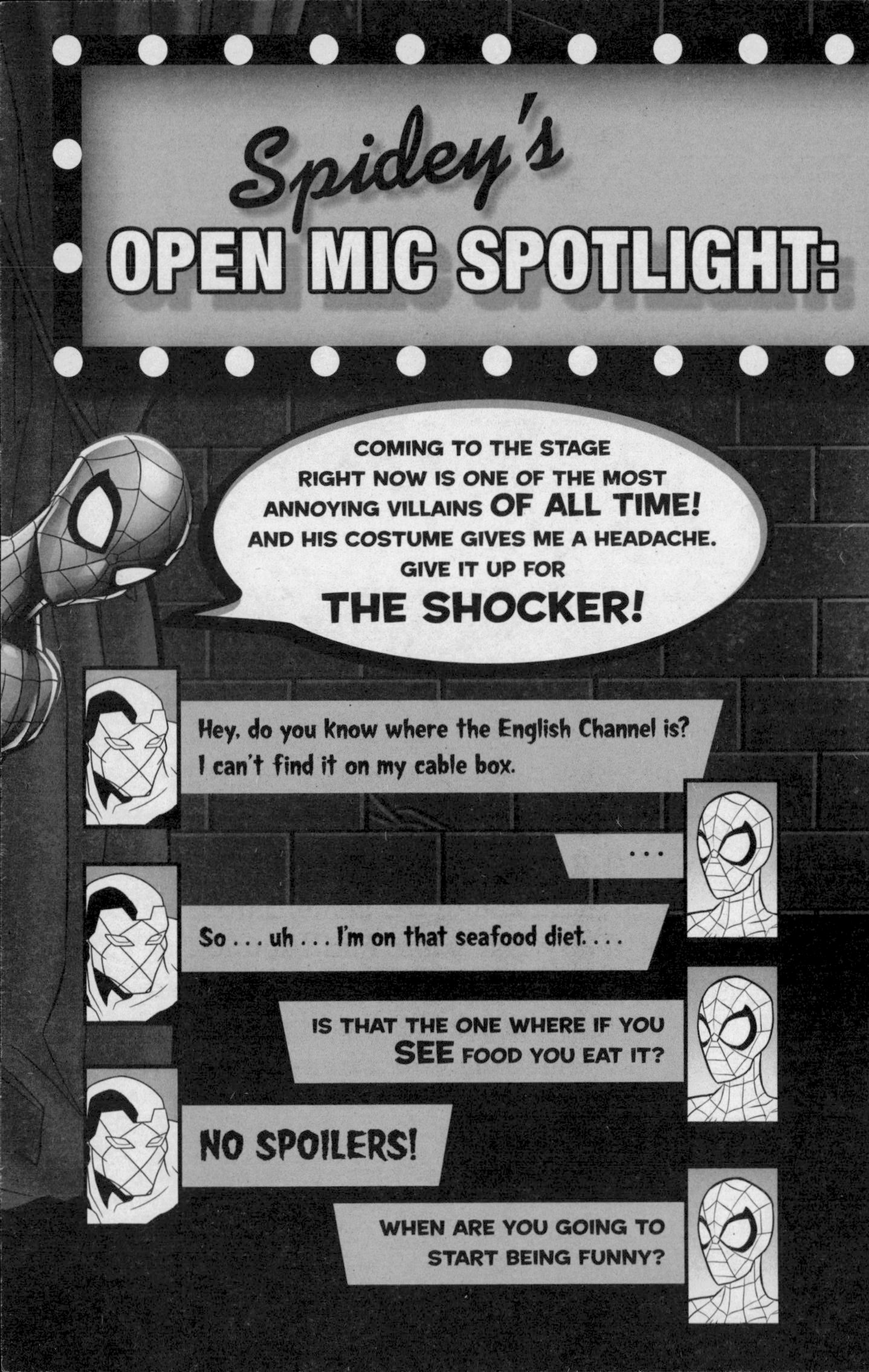
Spidey's
OPEN MIC SPOTLIGHT:
COMING TO THE STAGE RIGHT NOW IS ONE OF THE MOST ANNOYING VILLAINS OF ALL TIME! AND HIS COSTUME GIVES ME A HEADACHE. GIVE IT UP FOR THE SHOCKER!
Hey, do you know where the English Channel is? I can't find it on my cable box.
. . .
So . . . uh . . . I'm on that seafood diet. . . .
IS THAT THE ONE WHERE IF YOU SEE FOOD YOU EAT IT?
NO SPOILERS!
WHEN ARE YOU GOING TO START BEING FUNNY?

The Shocker

Hey, you better pipe down over there! Guess what, web-slinger? YO MAMA loves food SO MUCH that she eats A LOT of it . . . and . . . um . . . sorry. I messed that one up. DARN IT. I'm not so great at this after all.

SHOCKER!

Yes?

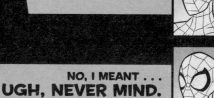

NO, I MEANT . . .
UGH, NEVER MIND.

WHEN YOU'RE A SUPER LIFE KEEPS PUNCHING

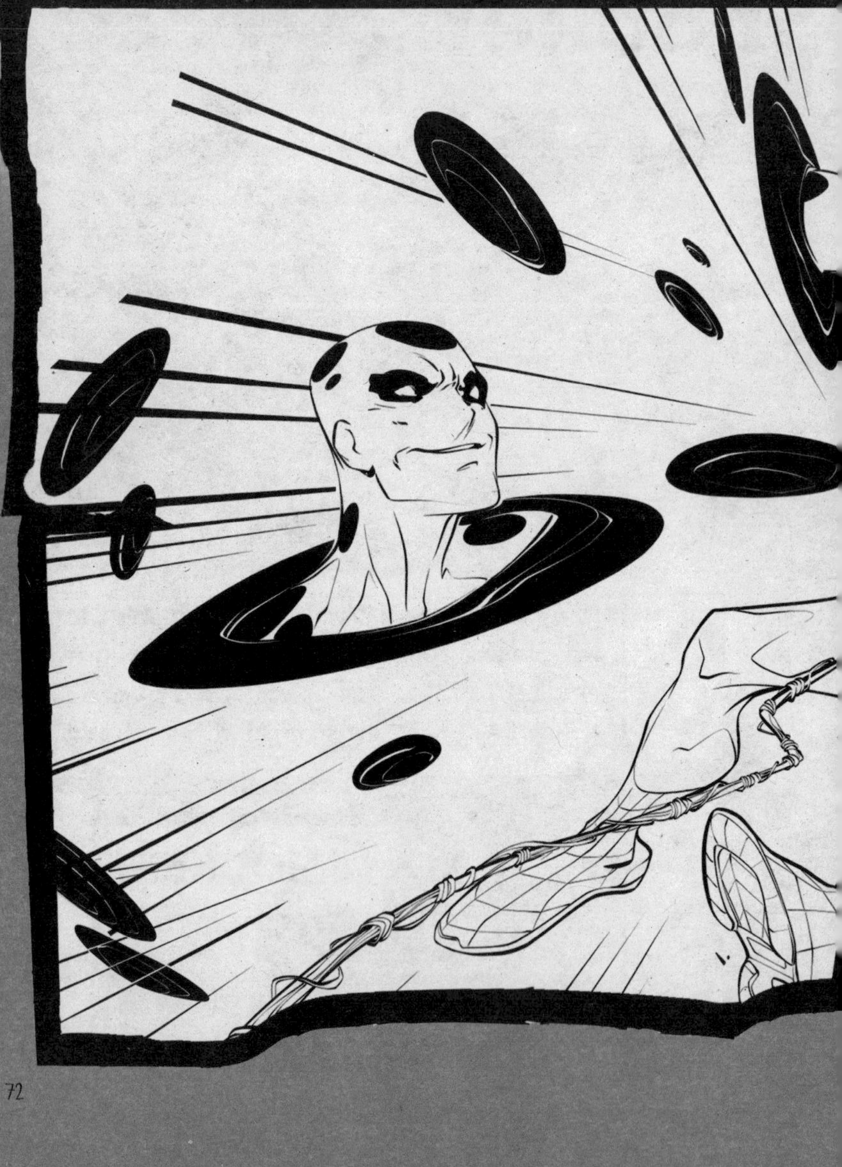

HERO BUT SOMEHOW
YOU IN THE FACE

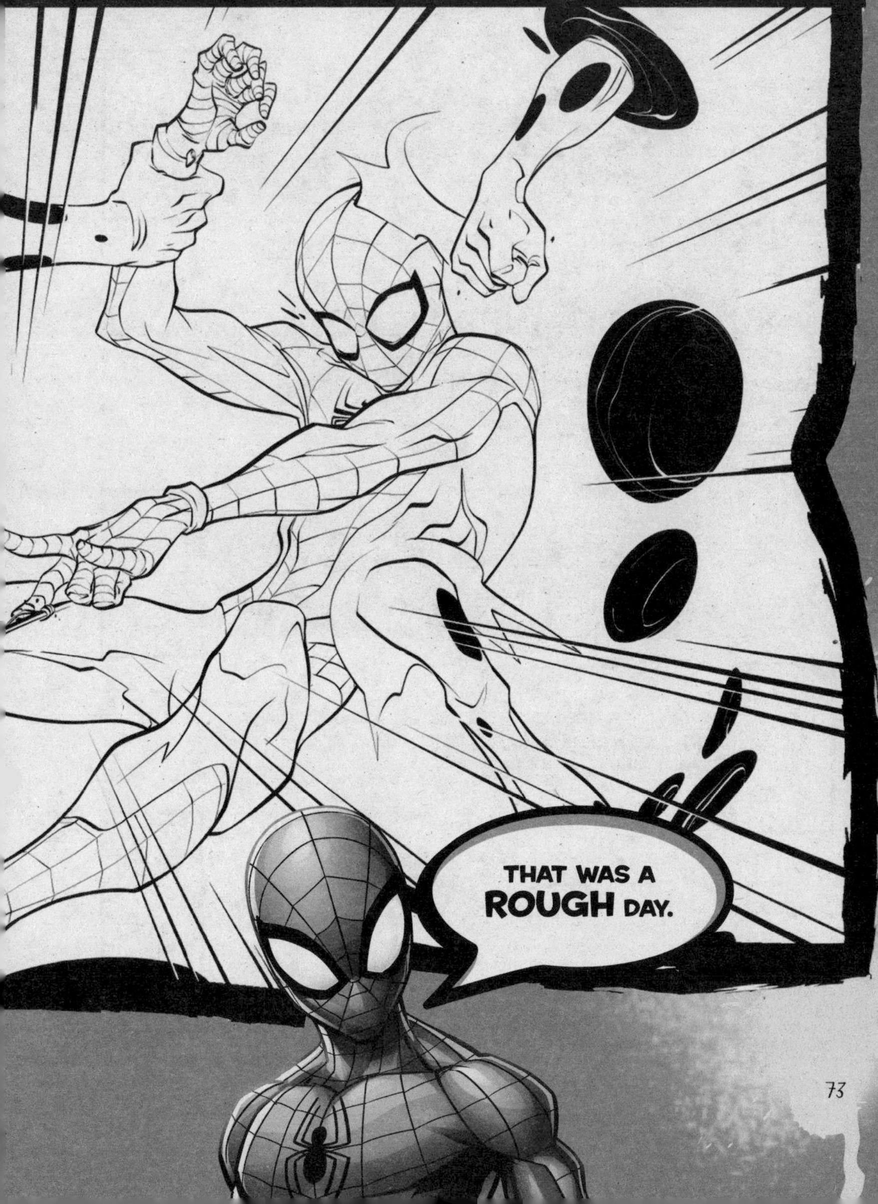
THAT WAS A ROUGH DAY.

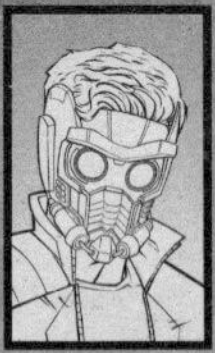

The GUARDIANS OF THE GALAXY are here to lay down some serious funny business.

HEY, STAR-LORD! UM, IN CASE YOU DIDN'T KNOW, THIS IS **MY** JOKE BOOK. I'LL DO THE INTRODUCTIONS AROUND HERE.

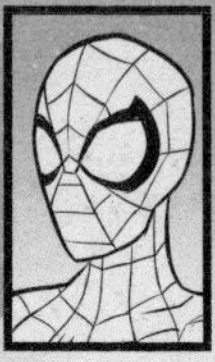

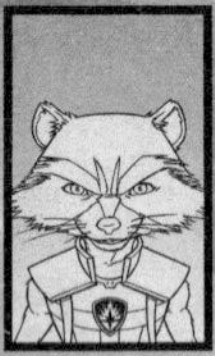

BEAT IT, WEB HEAD! It's our time to shine. Take it away, Gamora. . . .

What do you call a pig that does karate?

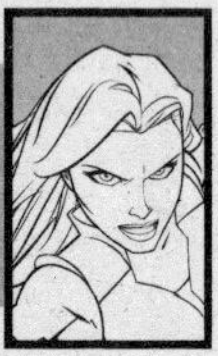

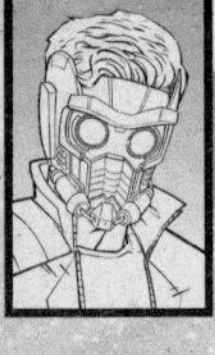

A pork chop!

See? Now **THAT'S** comedy.

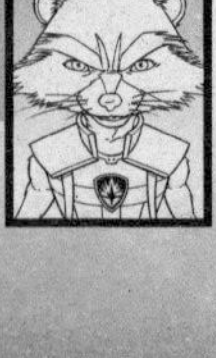

BUT THIS IS MY GIG. I'M THE DUDE WHO MAKES THE FUNNY!

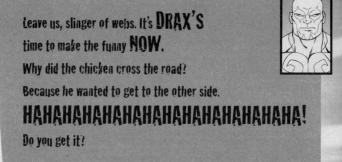

Leave us, slinger of webs. It's **DRAX'S** time to make the funny **NOW**.

Why did the chicken cross the road?

Because he wanted to get to the other side.

HAHAHAHAHAHAHAHAHAHAHAHAHAHAHA!

Do you get it?

Eh. Okay, so **maybe** we have some work to do.

I AM GROOT!

GOOD LUCK, YOU GUYS. (YOU'RE GOING TO NEED IT.)

Q: Why was the salad naked?
A: The server forgot to bring the dressing.

Q: What's a boulder's favorite type of music?
A: Rock 'n' roll.

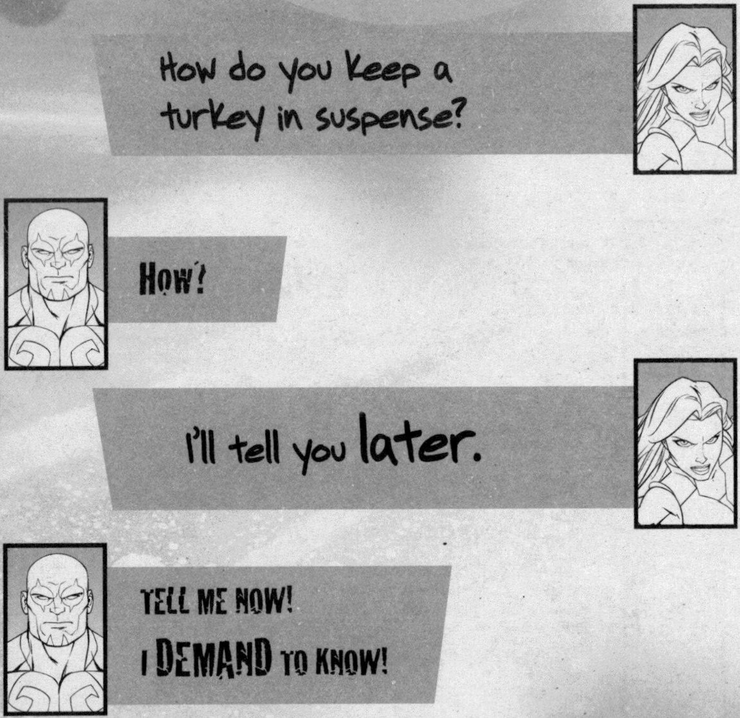
How do you keep a turkey in suspense?
How?
I'll tell you later.
TELL ME NOW! I DEMAND TO KNOW!

Q: Why was the tree excited
   about the future?
A: It was ready to turn over
   a new leaf!

Q: Why did the pie go to the dentist?
A: It needed a filling.

Q: What did the earthquake say to
   the tornado?
A: It's not my fault!

Q: What's a plumber's favorite vegetable?
A: A leek.

Q: What did the traffic light say to
   the car?
A: Don't look now, I'm changing.

Q: Why is a chef the most violent job around?
A: Because they beat eggs and whip cream.

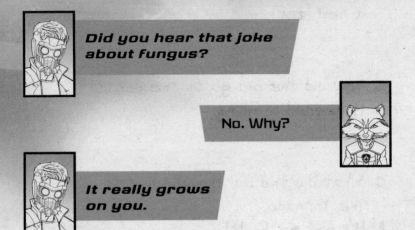

Did you hear that joke about fungus?

No. Why?

It really grows on you.

Q: What did the grape say
   when DRAX stepped on it?
A: It let out a little whine.

Q: What instrument does a cucumber play?
A: A pickle-lo.

Q: Did you hear about the angry pancake?
A: He totally flipped.

WHEN YOU'RE WAY TOO GOOD-LOOKING FOR THIS JOKE BOOK

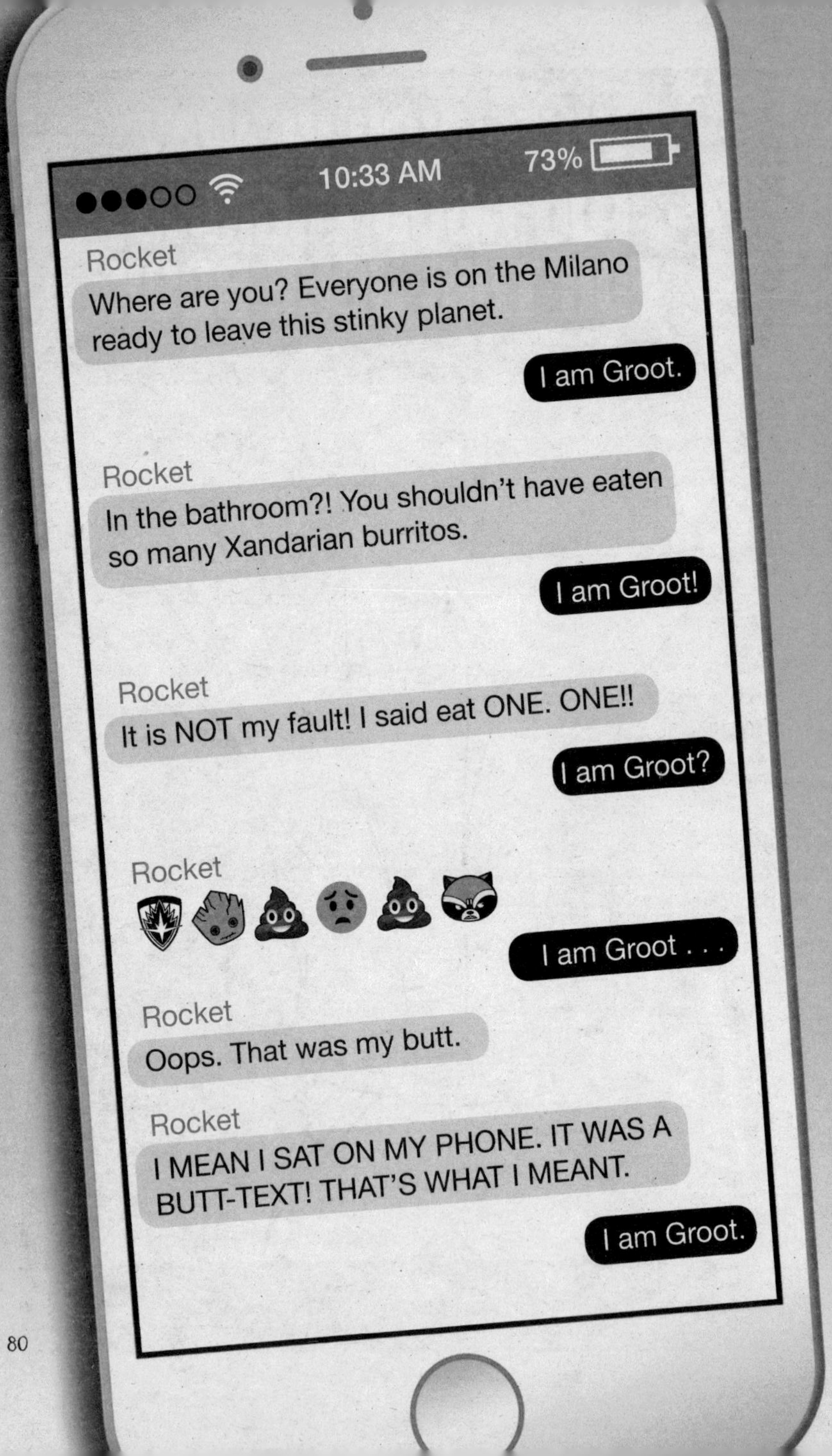
10:33 AM
73%
Rocket
Where are you? Everyone is on the Milano ready to leave this stinky planet.
I am Groot.
Rocket
In the bathroom?! You shouldn't have eaten so many Xandarian burritos.
I am Groot!
Rocket
It is NOT my fault! I said eat ONE. ONE!!
I am Groot?
Rocket
I am Groot . . .
Rocket
Oops. That was my butt.
Rocket
I MEAN I SAT ON MY PHONE. IT WAS A BUTT-TEXT! THAT'S WHAT I MEANT.
I am Groot.

Q: Where does a pig store
   its money?
A: A piggy bank.

Q: What do you call a cow
   that's afraid of everything?
A: A cow-ard.

Q: What kind of car does Rocket drive?
A: A Furrari.

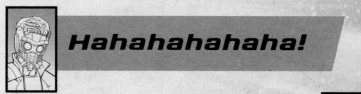

Hahahahahahaha!

I don't get it.

Q: Why are cats terrible storytellers?
A: They only have one tail.

Q: What do you get when you cross a pig with a centipede?

A: Bacon and legs.

Q: What kind of cat should you never play games with?

A: A cheetah.

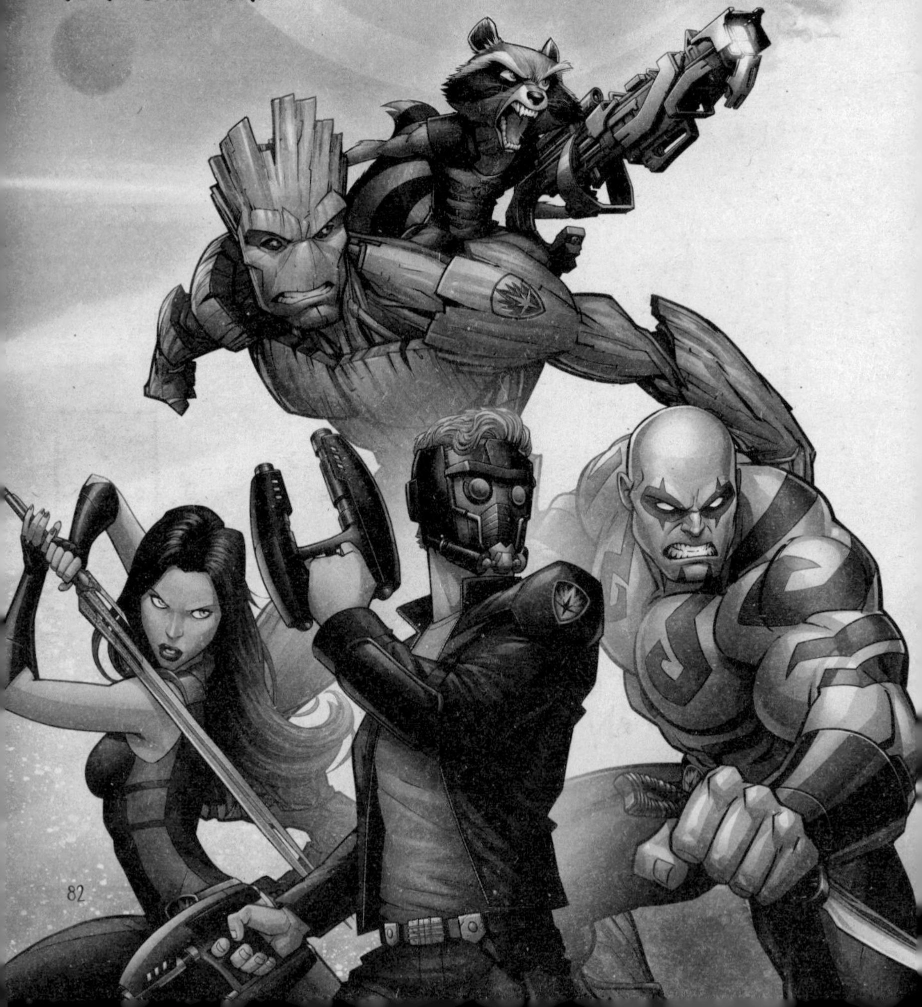

Q: What did the duck say when it bought lipstick?
A: Put it on my bill.

Q: What do you get from a pampered cow?
A: Spoiled milk.

Q: What's the most musical part of a chicken?
A: The drumstick!

Q: Why didn't the butterfly go to the dance?
A: It was a mothball.

Q: Did you hear that Black Panther got 100 percent on a test?
A: It was a purrfect score.

Q: What lion never roars?
A: A dandeLION!

Q: HOW DOES GROOT GET ON THE INTERNET?

A: **HE LOGS ON!**

Q: WHAT DOES GROOT WEAR TO THE POOL PARTY?

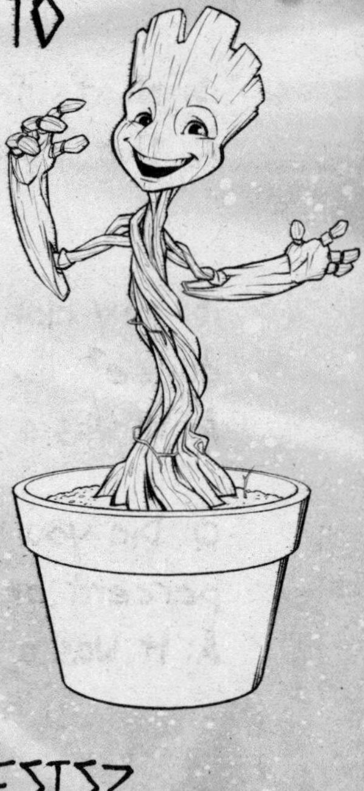

A: **SWIMMING TRUNKS!**

Q: WHAT'S GROOT'S FAVORITE SODA?

A: **ROOT BEER!**

Q: WHY DOES GROOT HATE TESTS?

A: **HE USUALLY GETS STUMPED!**

WHEN YOUR FRIEND SAYS "I AM GROOT"

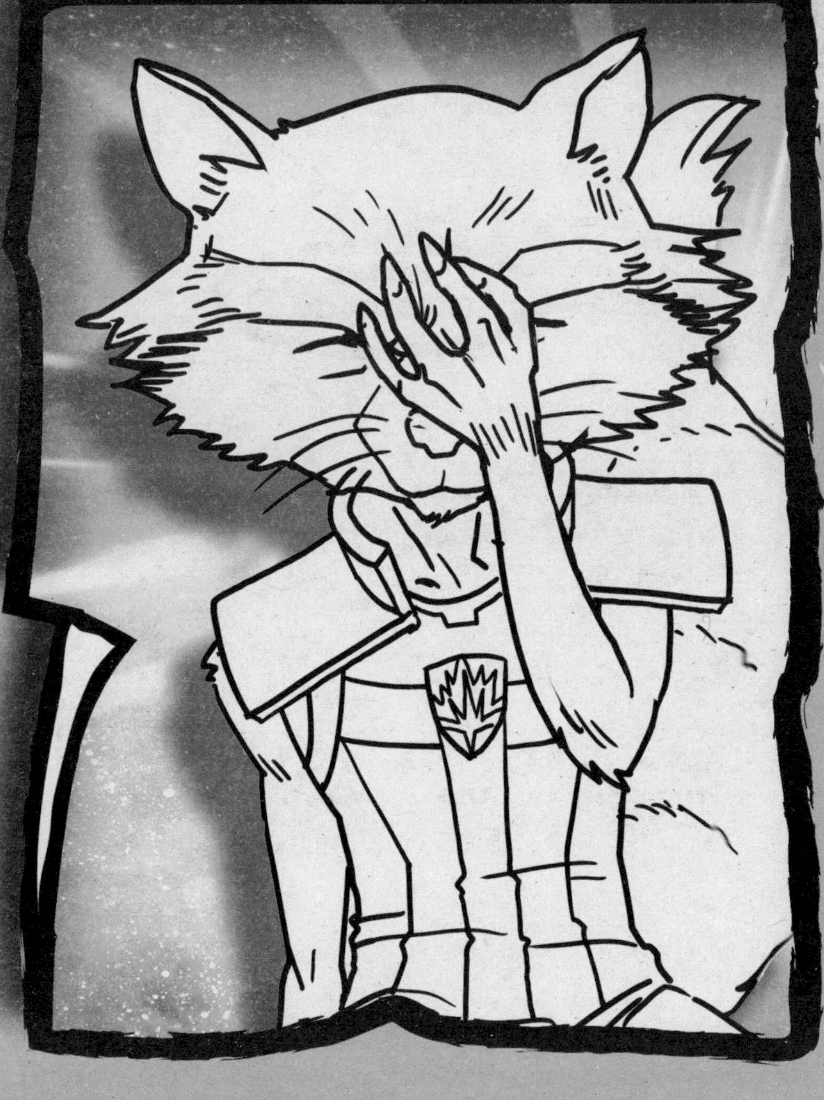

YO MAMA's glasses are so thick, she can see into the future!

 You better watch what you say about my MAMA, fur ball!

 OH NO. HERE WE GO.

 YO MAMA is so weird, she walked into a haunted house, and they offered her a job!

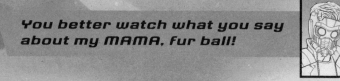 YO MAMA is so lazy, she stuck her nose out the window to let the wind blow it!

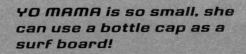

YO MAMA's feet so big, her sneakers need license plates.

YO MAMA is so small, she can use a bottle cap as a surf board!

YO MAMA is so silly, she put her air conditioner in backward so she could chill outside!

YO MAMA is so mean, she threw a boomerang and it never came back!

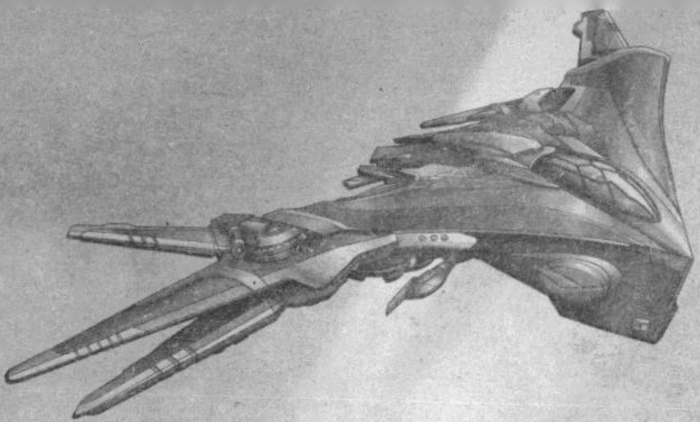

EVERY DAY I'M

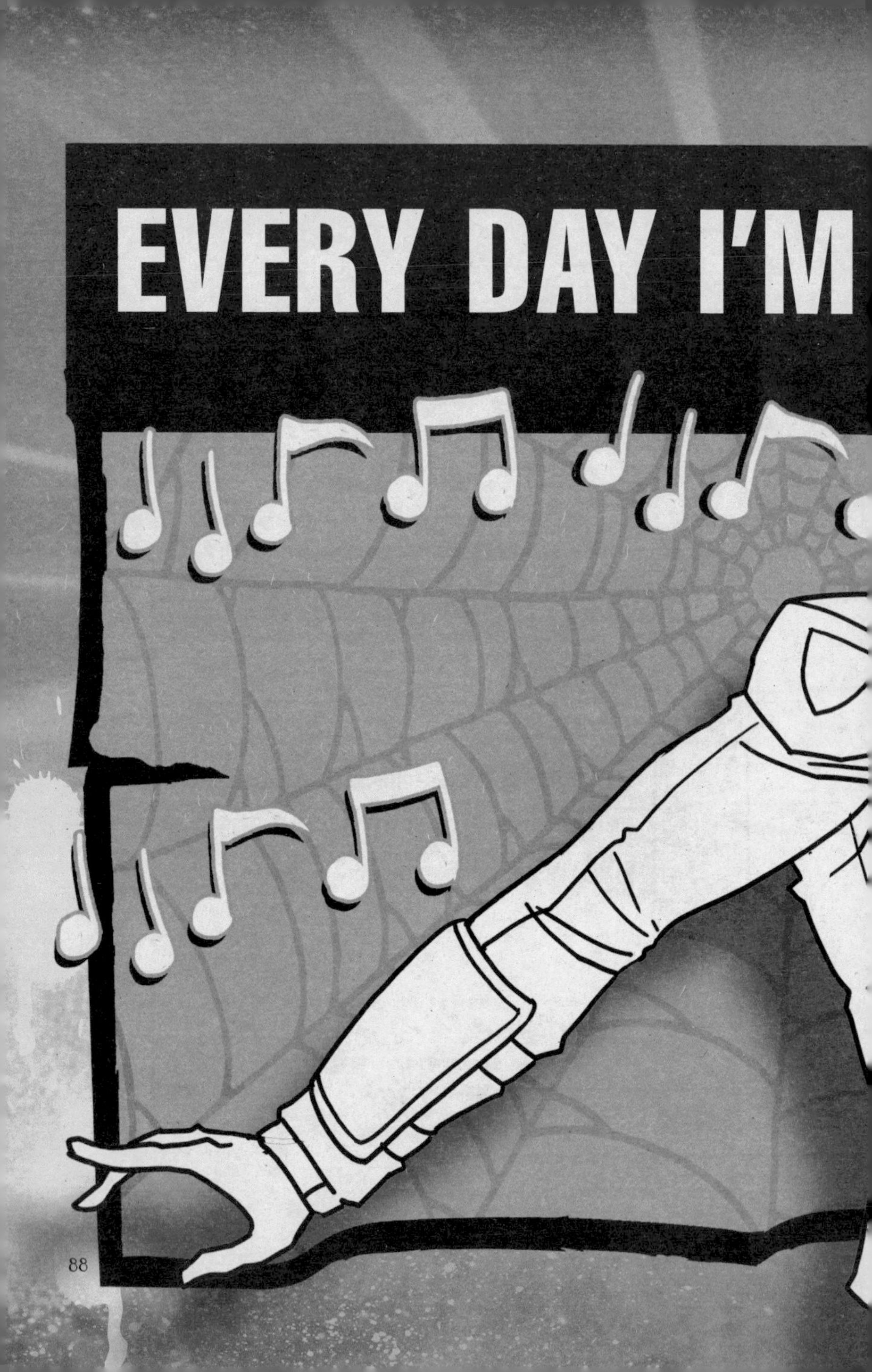

SHUFFLIN'

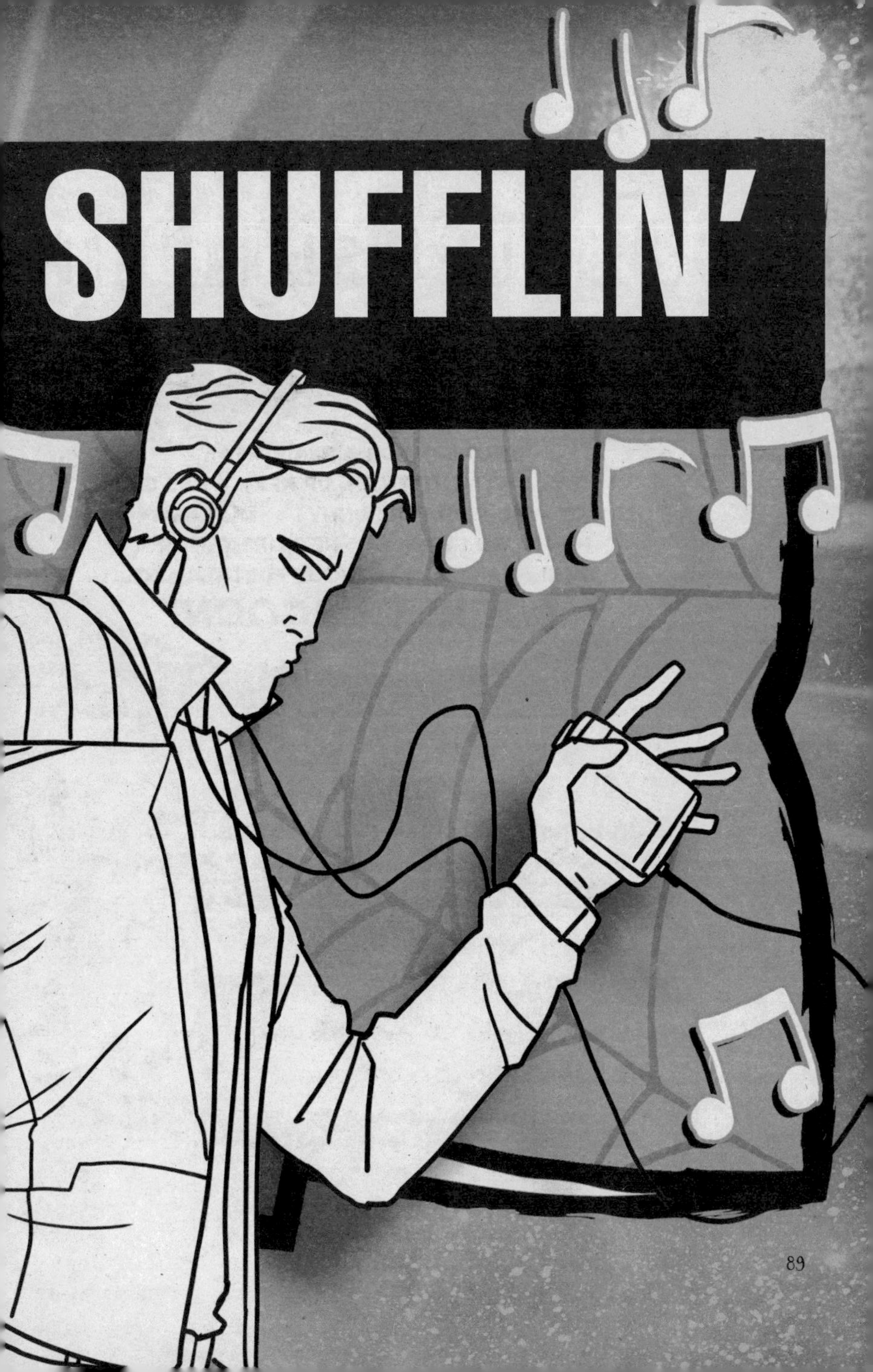

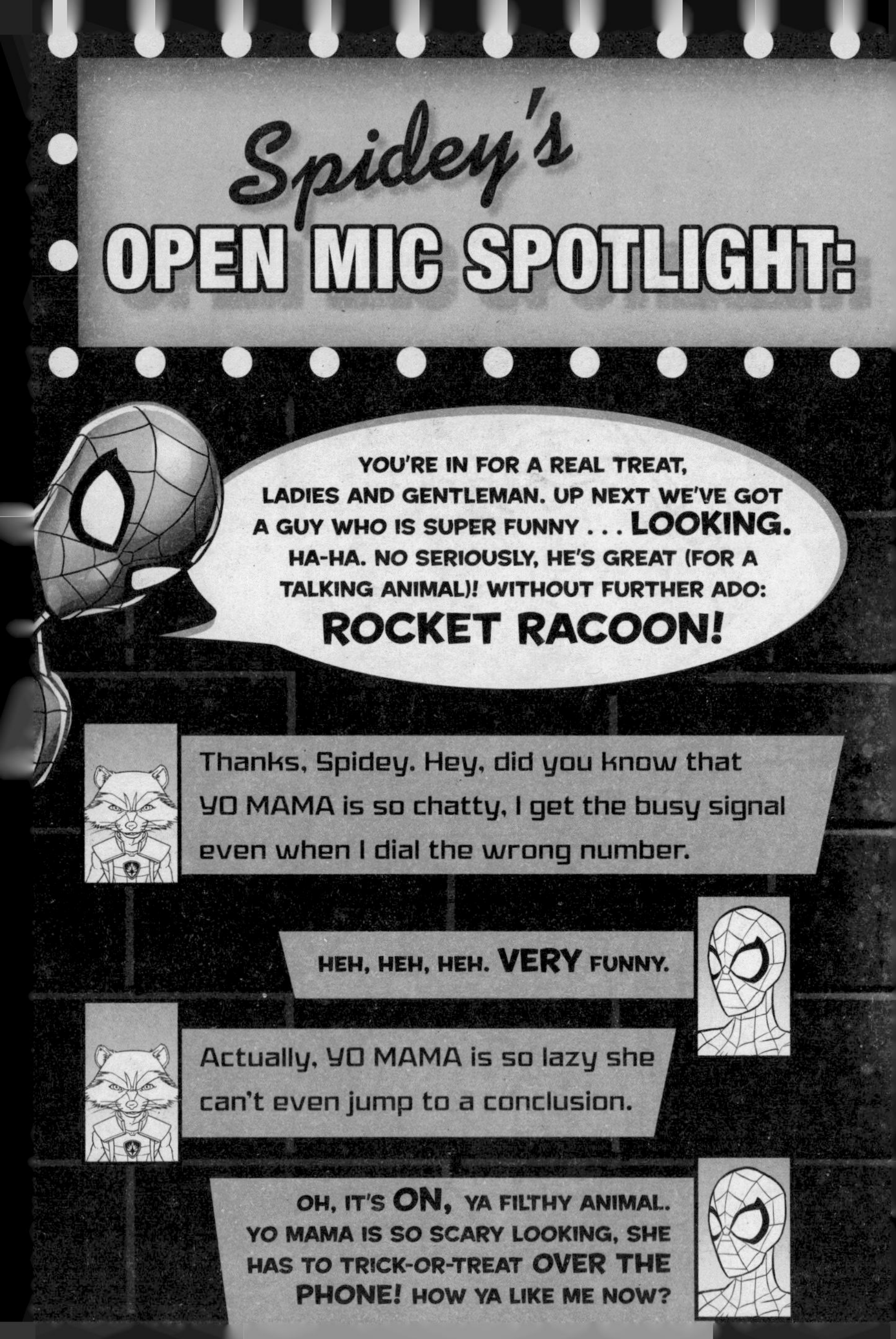
Spidey's
OPEN MIC SPOTLIGHT:
YOU'RE IN FOR A REAL TREAT, LADIES AND GENTLEMAN. UP NEXT WE'VE GOT A GUY WHO IS SUPER FUNNY . . . LOOKING. HA-HA. NO SERIOUSLY, HE'S GREAT (FOR A TALKING ANIMAL)! WITHOUT FURTHER ADO: ROCKET RACOON!
Thanks, Spidey. Hey, did you know that YO MAMA is so chatty, I get the busy signal even when I dial the wrong number.
HEH, HEH, HEH. VERY FUNNY.
Actually, YO MAMA is so lazy she can't even jump to a conclusion.
OH, IT'S ON, YA FILTHY ANIMAL. YO MAMA IS SO SCARY LOOKING, SHE HAS TO TRICK-OR-TREAT OVER THE PHONE! HOW YA LIKE ME NOW?

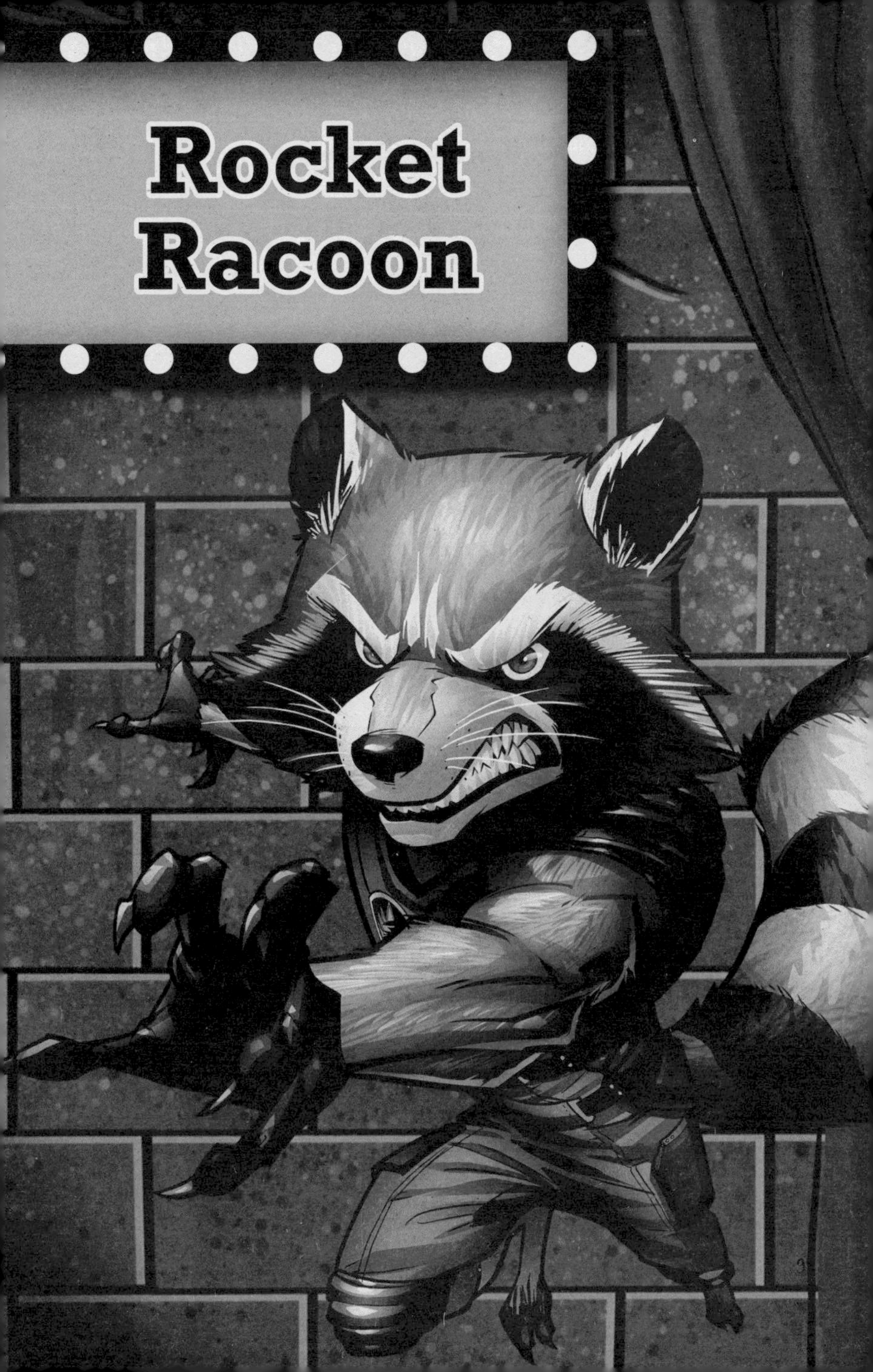
Rocket
Racoon

What did the tree say to the wind?

Hmmm. I need to branch out?

Leaf me alone?

I AM GROOOOOT!

One last thing, Spider-Man. How do you plan a space party?

I HAVE **NO** IDEA.

You **PLANET EARLY.**
(MIC DROP)

I WILL NOT MISS YOU GUYS WHEN THIS IS OVER.

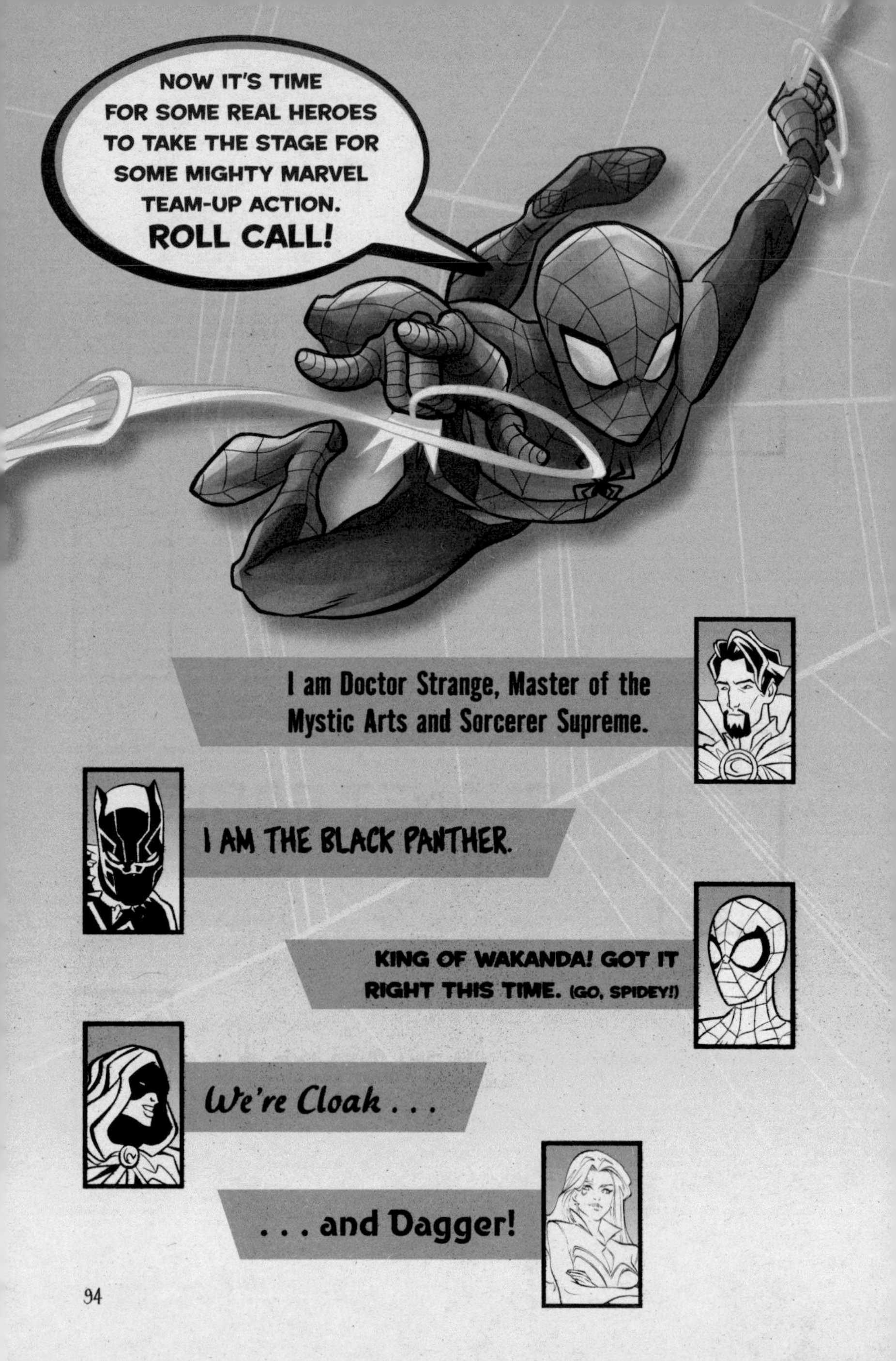
NOW IT'S TIME FOR SOME REAL HEROES TO TAKE THE STAGE FOR SOME MIGHTY MARVEL TEAM-UP ACTION. ROLL CALL!
I am Doctor Strange, Master of the Mystic Arts and Sorcerer Supreme.
I AM THE BLACK PANTHER.
KING OF WAKANDA! GOT IT RIGHT THIS TIME. (GO, SPIDEY!)
We're Cloak . . .
. . . and Dagger!

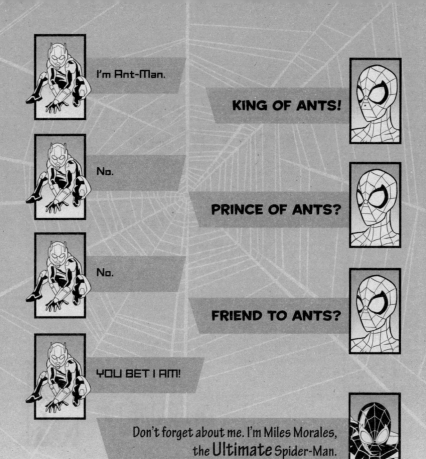

I'm Ant-Man.

KING OF ANTS!

No.

PRINCE OF ANTS?

No.

FRIEND TO ANTS?

YOU BET I AM!

Don't forget about me. I'm Miles Morales, the Ultimate Spider-Man.

GOOD TO SEE YOU, KID, BUT NOTHING BEATS THE ORIGINAL.

You're AMAZING, but Miles is THE ULTIMATE. He wins.

MIND YOUR ANTS, DUDE!

Q: HOW DOES BLACK PANTHER DO HIS SHOPPING?

A: FROM A **CAT**-A-LOG.

Q: WHAT'S BLACK PANTHER'S FAVORITE COLOR?

A: **PURRR**PLE.

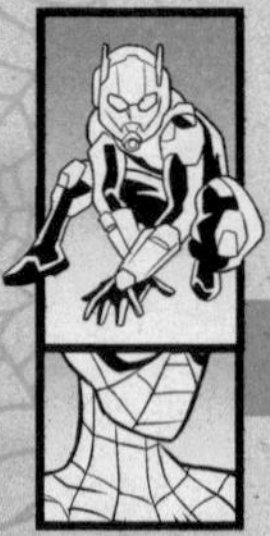

HOW'S IT GOING, BLACK PANTHER?

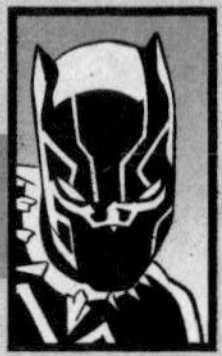

I'M **FELINE** FINE.

Q: WHAT DO YOU CALL BLACK PANTHER WHEN HE'S HAVING A BAD DAY?

A: A SOUR **PUSS**.

Q: What does Ant-Man take when he's sick?
A: ANTibiotics.

Q: What do you get when you cross Ant-Man with some ticks?
A: ANTics!

I'm sensing a theme.

YOU'RE BRILLIANT!

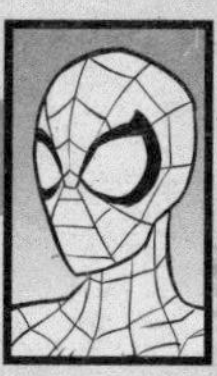

Q: What do you call Ant-Man when he turns one hundred?
A: An ANTique.

Q: What does Ant-Man eat for breakfast?
A: CroissANTs.

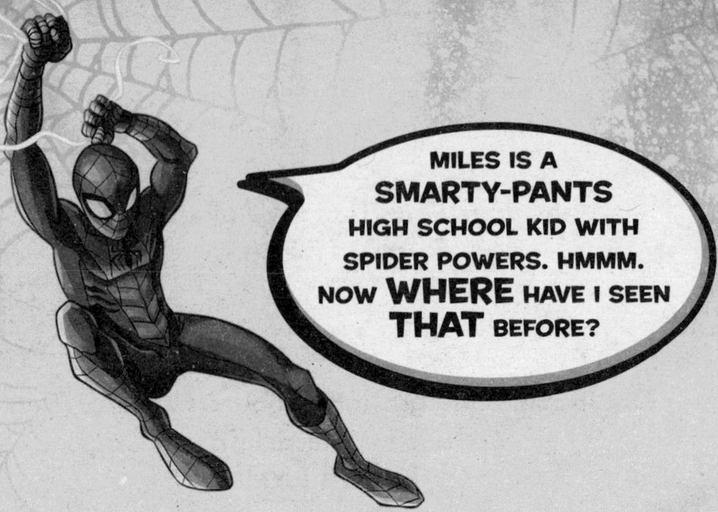
MILES IS A SMARTY-PANTS HIGH SCHOOL KID WITH SPIDER POWERS. HMMM. NOW WHERE HAVE I SEEN THAT BEFORE?

Q: Why did the music teacher need a ladder?

A: To reach the high notes.

Q: What's the worst thing you're likely to find in the school cafeteria?

A: The food.

Q: What kind of hair do oceans have?

A: Wavy!

Q: What do librarians take with them when they go fishing?

A: Bookworms.

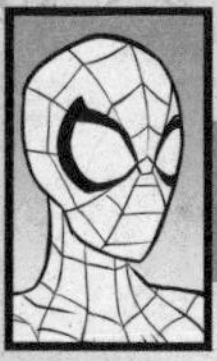

MILES, WHY WAS YOUR HOMEWORK SO SAD?

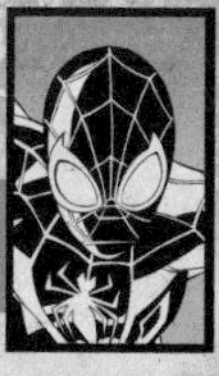

Because it had too many problems!

Q: Why didn't the sun go to college?

A: Because it already had a million degrees.

Q: What object is king of the classroom?

A: The ruler.

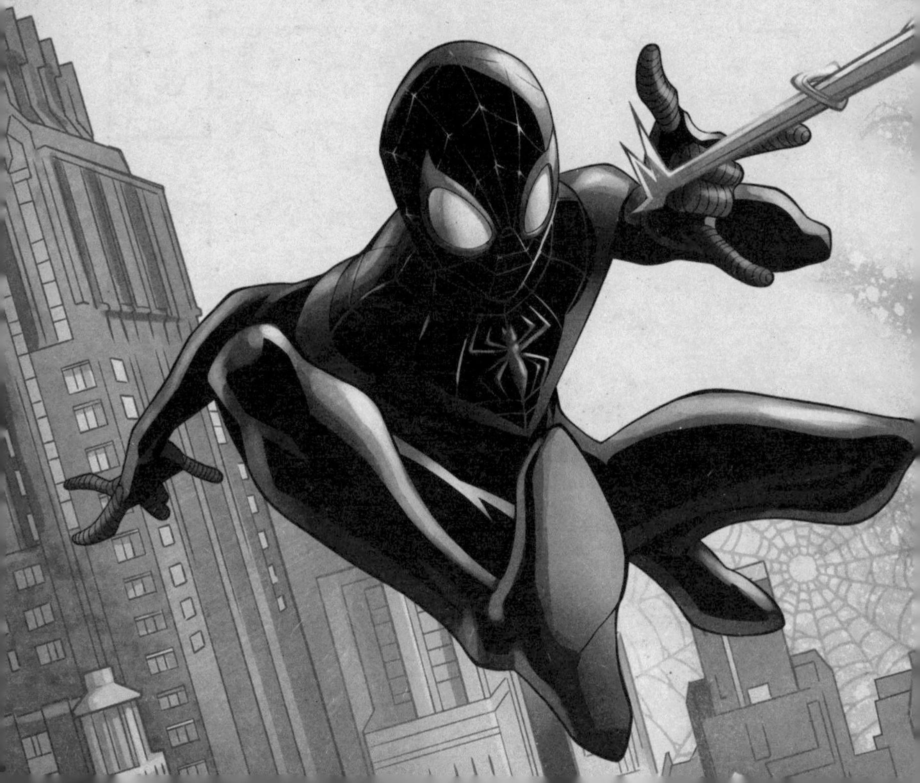

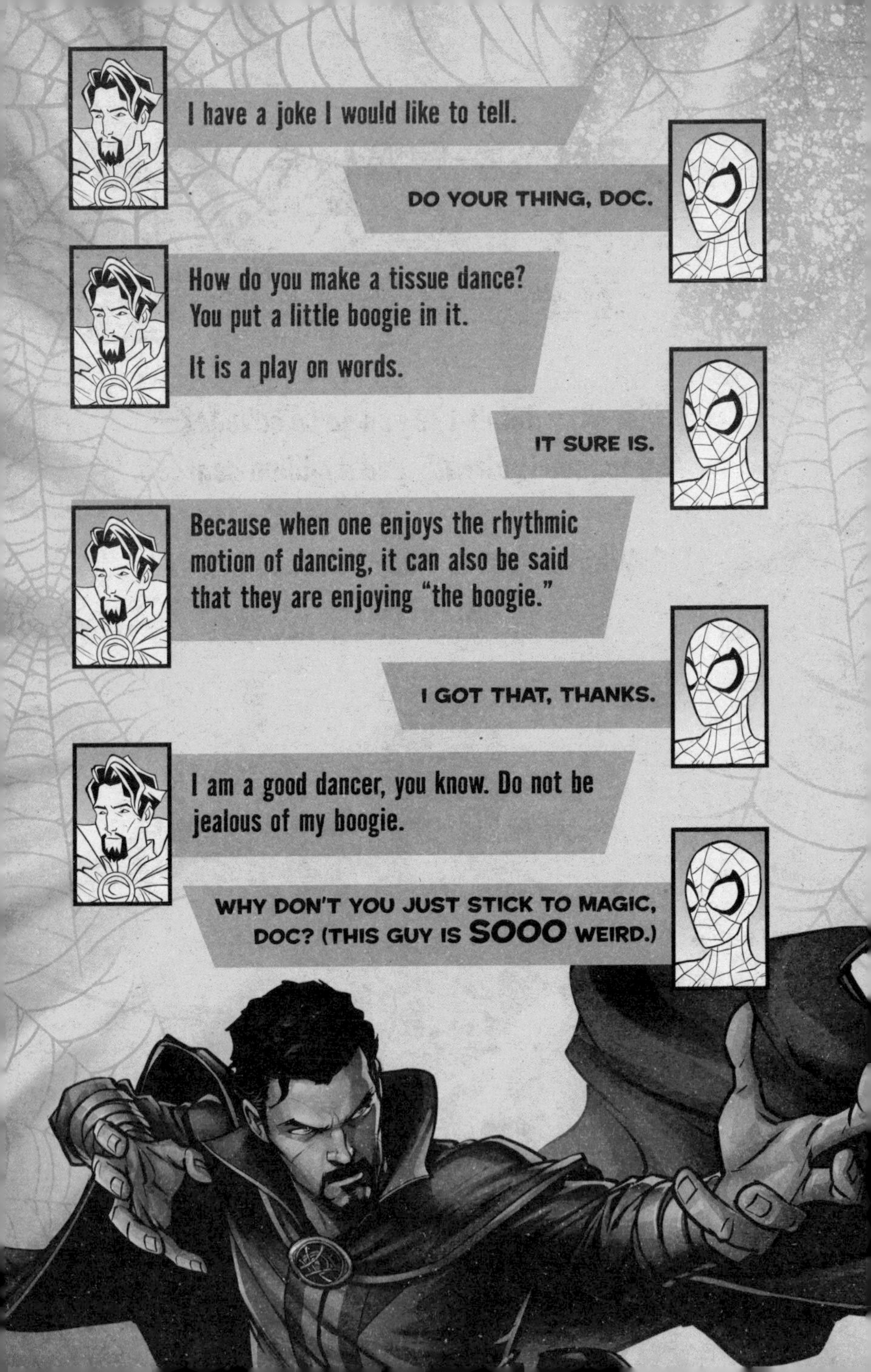
I have a joke I would like to tell.
DO YOUR THING, DOC.
How do you make a tissue dance? You put a little boogie in it.
It is a play on words.
IT SURE IS.
Because when one enjoys the rhythmic motion of dancing, it can also be said that they are enjoying "the boogie."
I GOT THAT, THANKS.
I am a good dancer, you know. Do not be jealous of my boogie.
WHY DON'T YOU JUST STICK TO MAGIC, DOC? (THIS GUY IS SOOO WEIRD.)

WHEN YOUR FRIENDS DON'T BELIEVE YOU HANG OUT WITH A RICH PRINCE SO YOU GOTTA SNAP A SELFIE FOR PROOF

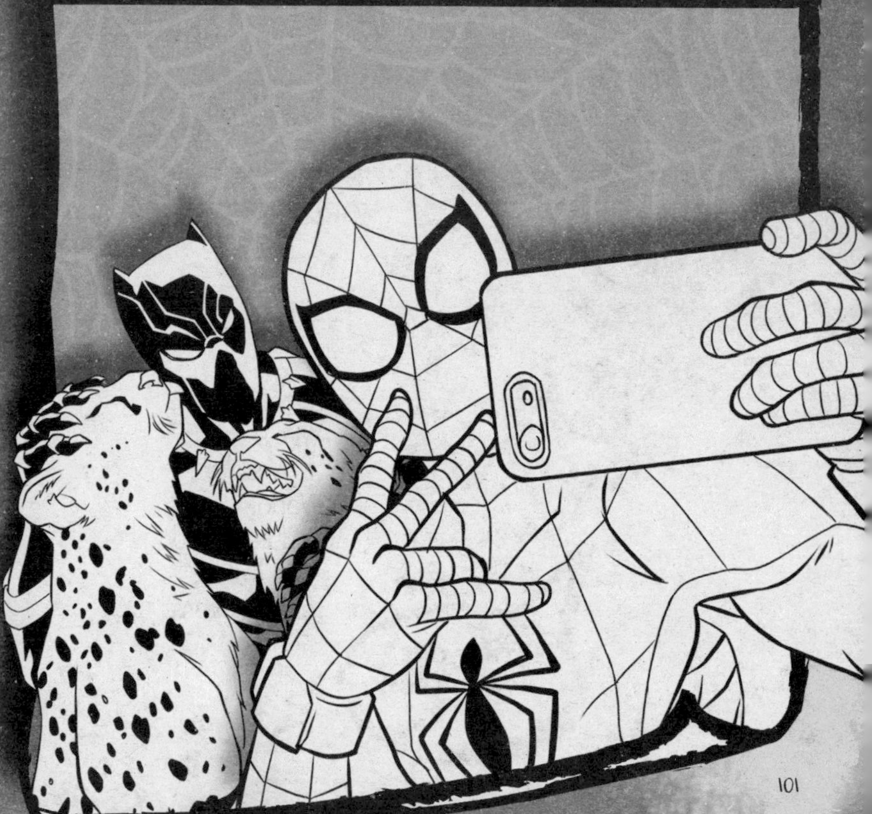

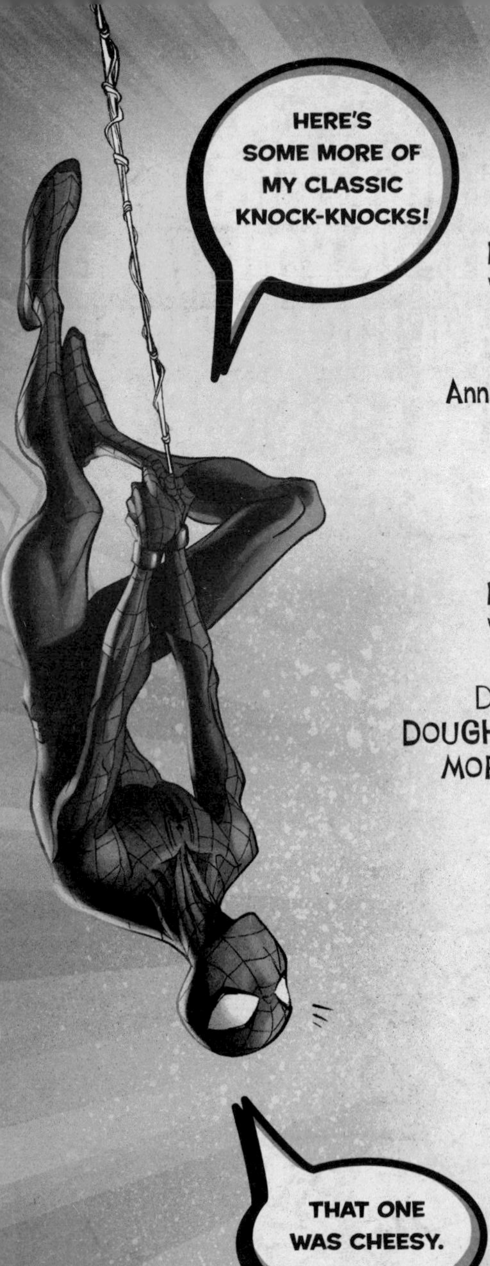
HERE'S SOME MORE OF MY CLASSIC KNOCK-KNOCKS!
THAT ONE WAS CHEESY.

Knock, knock.
Who's there?
Anna.
Anna who?
Anna one, Anna two,
Anna three!

Knock, knock.
Who's there?
Doughnut.
Doughnut who?
DOUGHNUT ASK ME ANY MORE QUESTIONS!

Knock, knock.
Who's there?
Waddle.
Waddle who?
Waddle you do
if I stop
telling jokes?

Knock, knock.
Who's there?
Queso.
Queso who?
Queso mistaken identity.

Knock, knock.
Who's there?
I am.
I am who?
You mean you don't know?

Knock, knock.
Who's there?
Yoda.
Yoda who?
Yoda weirdest person
I've ever met.

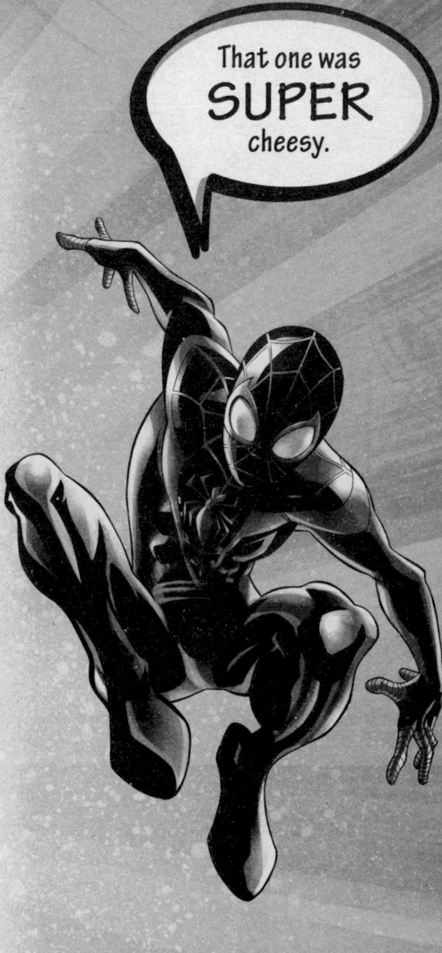
That one was SUPER cheesy.

Knock, knock.
Who's there?
Ken.
Ken who?
Ken you hear me now?

Knock, knock.
Who's there?
Alison.
Alison who?
Alison to you, but you have to listen to me first!

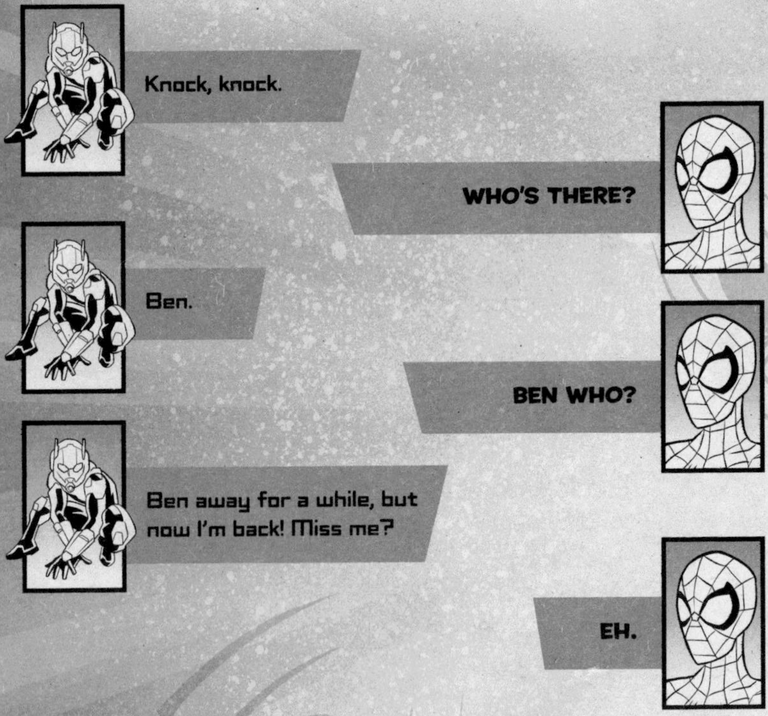

Knock, knock.
WHO'S THERE?
Ben.
BEN WHO?
Ben away for a while, but now I'm back! Miss me?
EH.

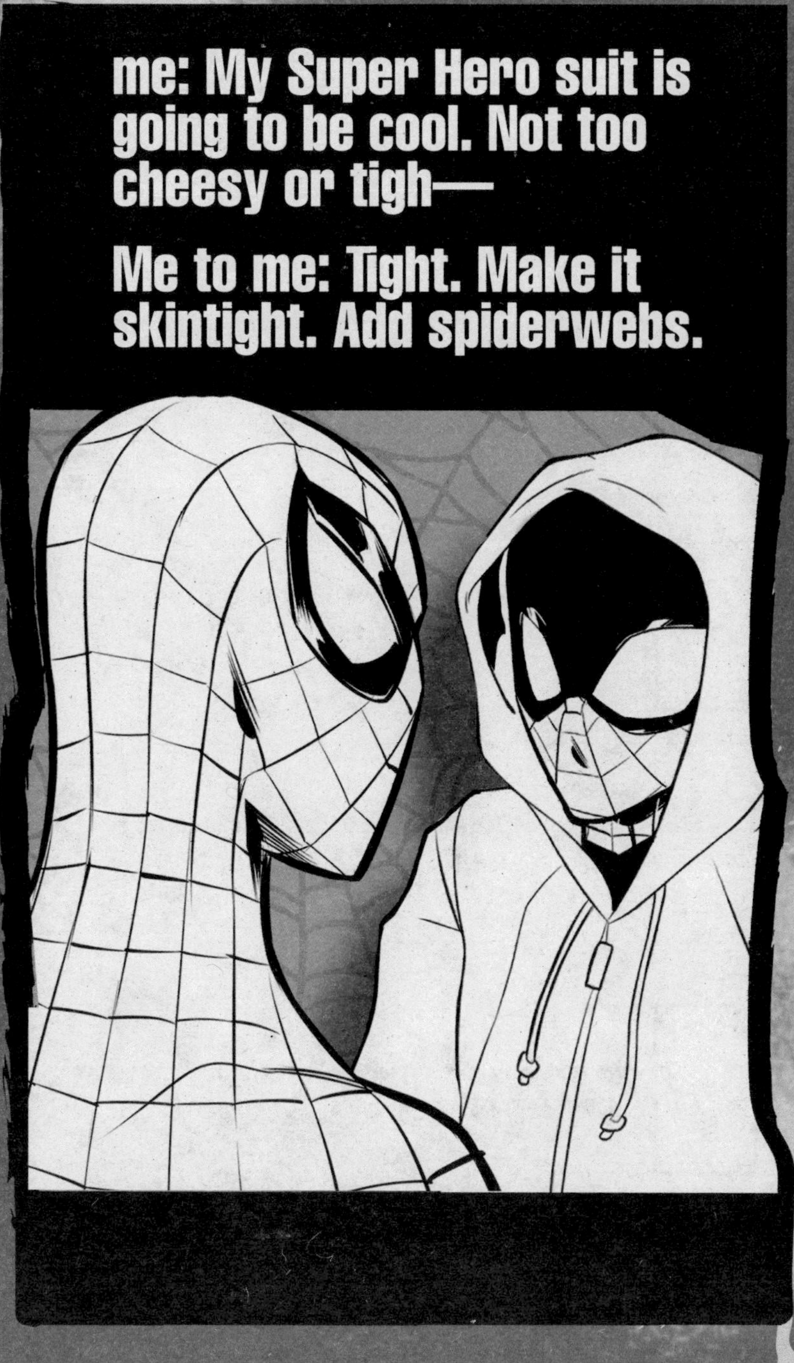
me: My Super Hero suit is going to be cool. Not too cheesy or tigh—
Me to me: Tight. Make it skintight. Add spiderwebs.

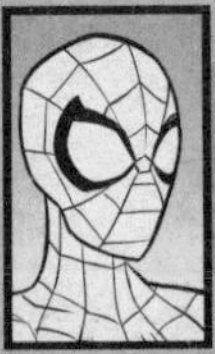

OH MAN. I DON'T KNOW IF I CAN TAKE ANY MORE **YO MAMA JOKES.**

Is it because YO MAMA is so silly she went to the beach to **surf** the **Internet?**

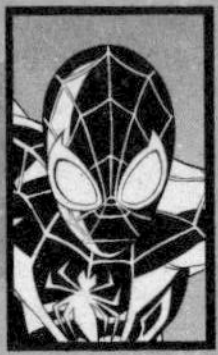

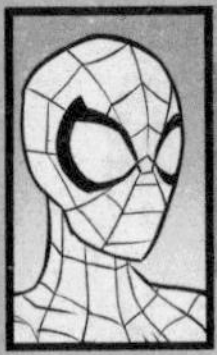

NO, IT'S BECAUSE YO MAMA IS SO BORING, I CAN'T THINK OF ANY MORE JOKES!

YO MAMA is so small, she can do **limbo under the door!**

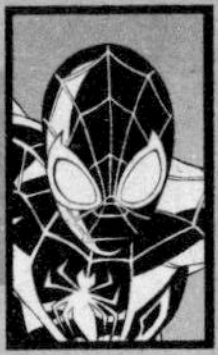

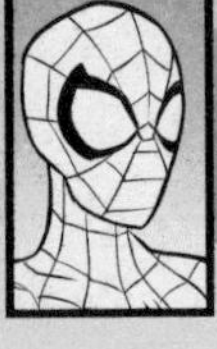

YO MAMA IS SO . . . NORMAL, SHE JUST SITS AT HOME AND LIVES HER LIFE!

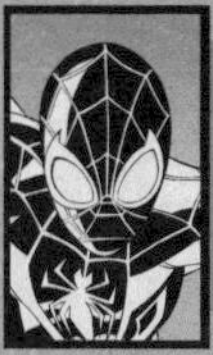

YO MAMA is so hungry, when she hears it's **chilly** outside she grabs a **spoon** and some **crackers**!

YO MAMA IS SO BUFF, SHE CAN DO THE BACKSTROKE IN MUD!

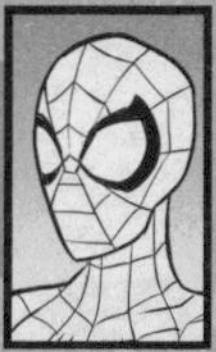

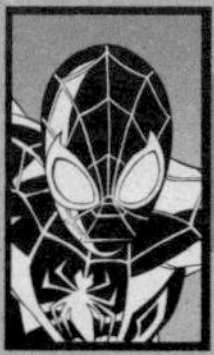

That last one was kind of a compliment.

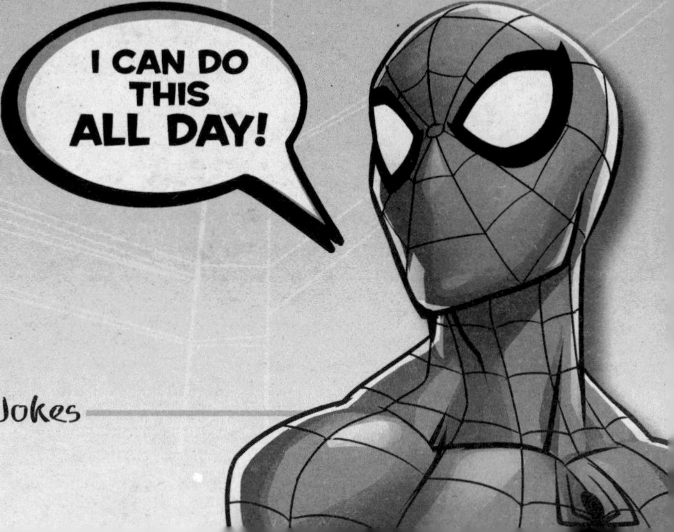
I CAN DO THIS ALL DAY!

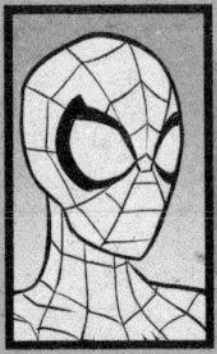

YO MAMA IS SO TINY THAT HER BEST FRIEND IS AN **ANT!**

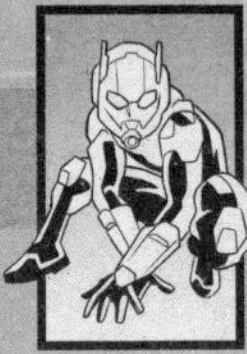

MY best friend is an ant.

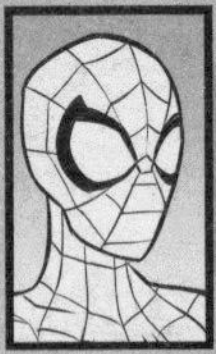

THIS GUY AND ANTS! GIVE IT A REST, WILL YOU? ANTS ARE COOL. **WE GET IT.**

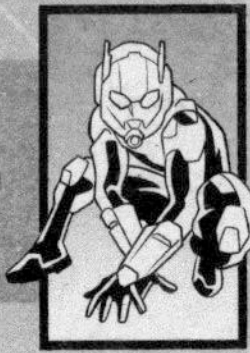

Do you? Do you get it? Because I heard YO MAMA is so big, when she turns around, her friends throw her a **"welcome back"** party!

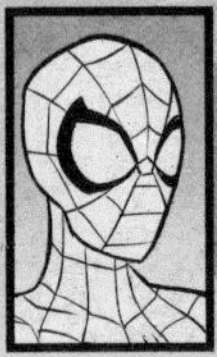

WOULDJA LOOK AT THAT. ANT-MAN IS **FINALLY** GETTING THE HANG OF THIS.

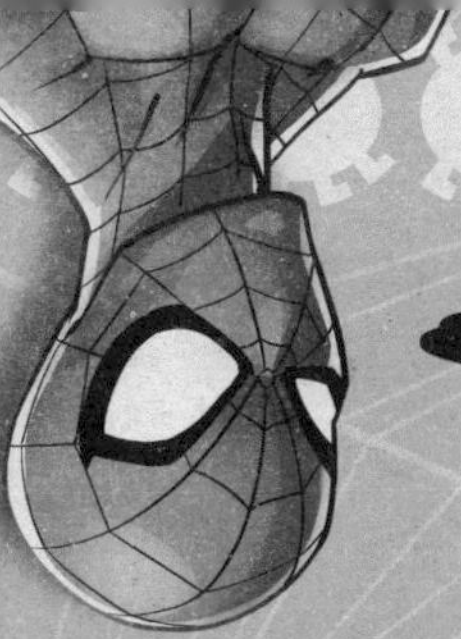
AND NOW . . .
CLOAK AND DAGGER
TELL A YO MAMA JOKE!

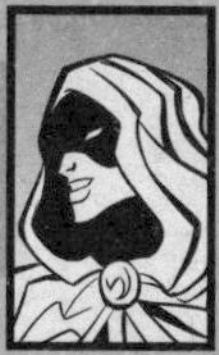

yo mama is so lazy . . .

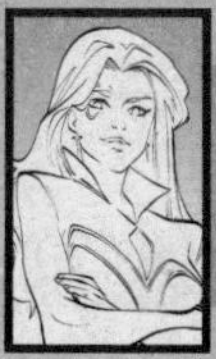

She has a stay-at-home job and still can't get to work on time!

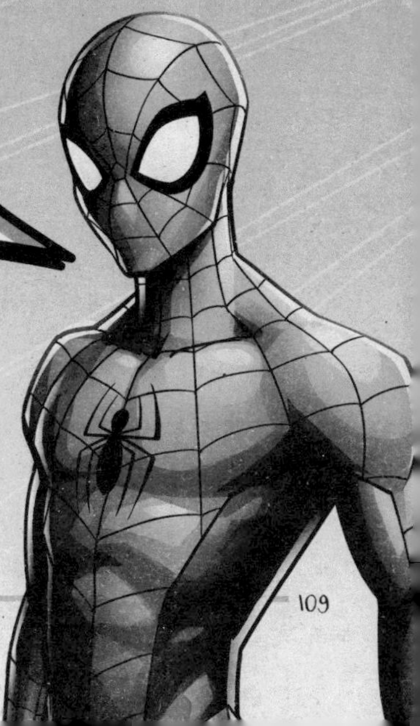
THIS HAS BEEN . . .
CLOAK AND DAGGER
TELL A
YO MAMA
JOKE!

Spider-Man
Hey, Groot! Are you coming to the party? It's insane! Everyone is asking about you. Doc Strange is wearing a lamp shade on his head already. It's hilarious.

I am Groot.

Spider-Man
You knew it was at 4:00 p.m. That's what the invite said! We need you here NOW, dude. You were in charge of bringing the chips and salsa!

I am Groot!

Spider-Man
I wasn't yelling. I was just being firm. I'm also dying of starvation. Listen, you're our buddy, and we all want you to come hang out.

I am Groot?

Spider-Man
Yes!

I am Groot!!!

Spider-Man
AWESOME. See you soon! And don't forget about those chips and salsa.

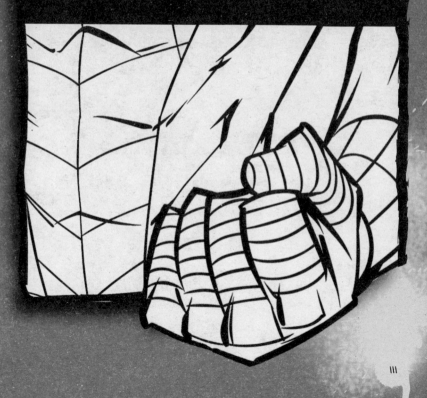

WHEN PEOPLE SAY "UNCLE BEN'S IS JUST A BRAND OF RICE"

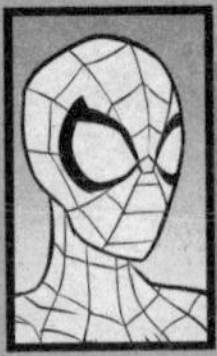

AND NOW THE MOMENT YOU'VE BEEN WAITING FOR . . . THE JOKE WALL AT THE END OF THE UNIVERSE!

I wasn't waiting for this moment. I'm kind of bored and need a nap! What about you, Black Panther?

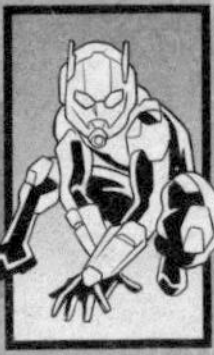

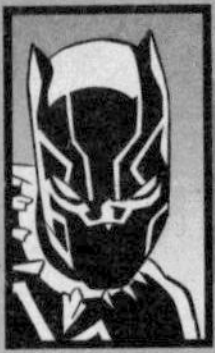

I FEEL THAT I HAVE DONE WHAT I CAME HERE TO DO AND AM FULFILLED.

YOU GUYS! I'M TRYING TO RUN A JOKE BOOK HERE, AND WE'RE ALMOST AT THE FINISH LINE. ARE YOU SURE YOU DON'T HAVE ONE MORE AWESOME JOKE IN YOU? PRETTY PLEASE?

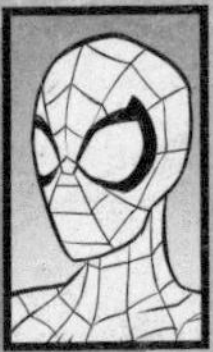

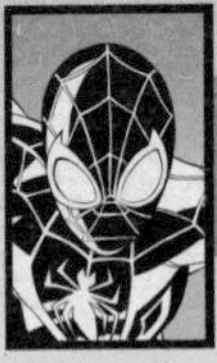

Sorry, Spidey. I've got homework.

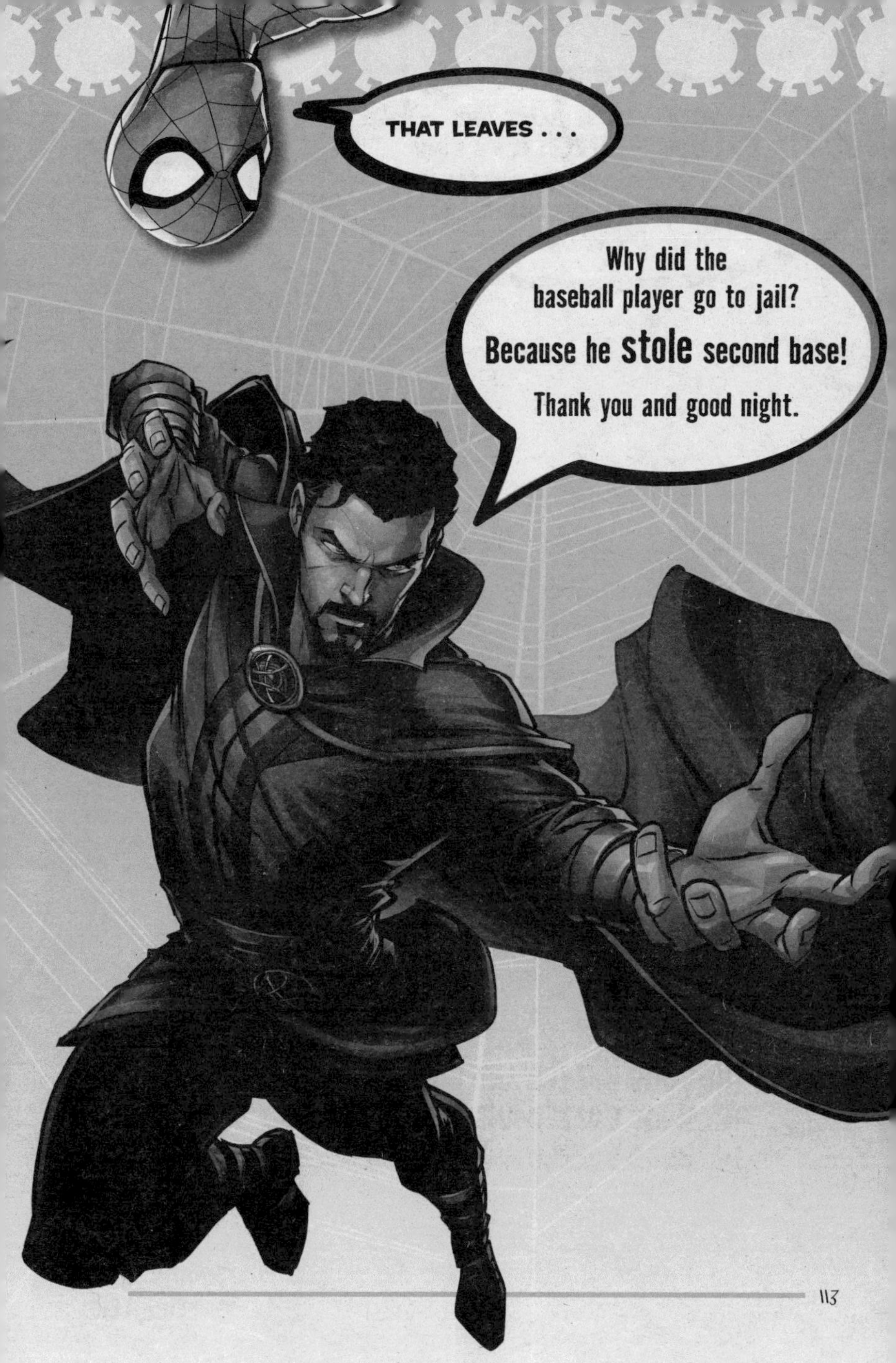
THAT LEAVES . . .
Why did the baseball player go to jail?
Because he stole second base!
Thank you and good night.

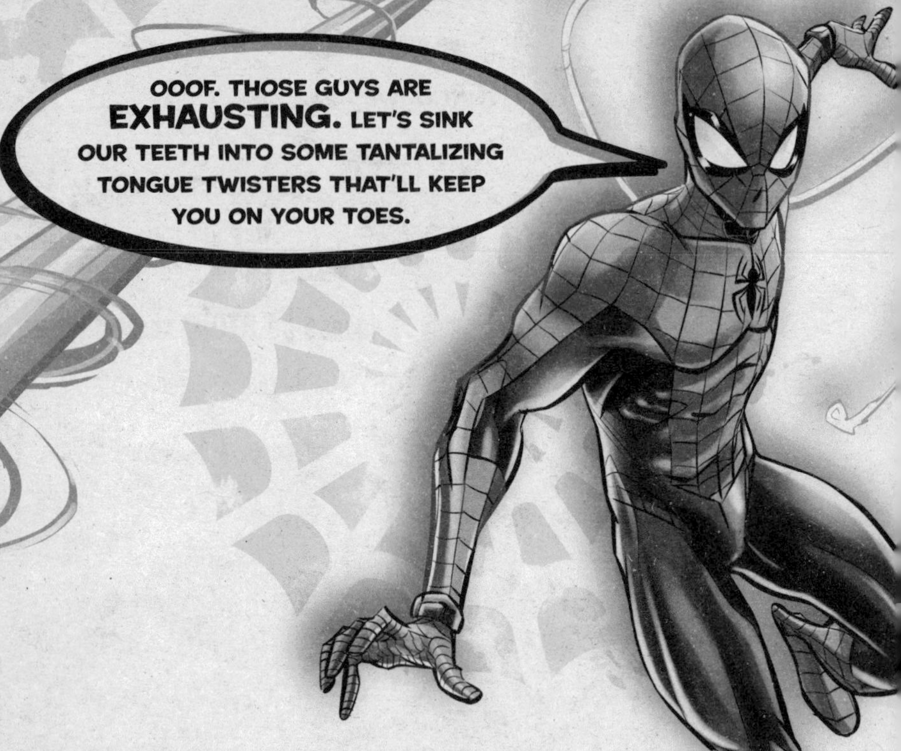
OOOF. THOSE GUYS ARE EXHAUSTING. LET'S SINK OUR TEETH INTO SOME TANTALIZING TONGUE TWISTERS THAT'LL KEEP YOU ON YOUR TOES.

SIX SICKLY SPIDERS SPUN SPECIAL SNARES.
SIX SICKLY SPIDERS SPUN SPECIAL SNARES.
SIX SICKLY SPIDERS SPUN SPECIAL SNARES.

THE BUGS BUZZED AND BUGGED BUZZ.
THE BUGS BUZZED AND BUGGED BUZZ.
THE BUGS BUZZED AND BUGGED BUZZ.

NO ONE KNEW HE KNEW WHAT HE KNEW.
NO ONE KNEW HE KNEW WHAT HE KNEW.
NO ONE KNEW HE KNEW WHAT HE KNEW.

TOY BOAT.
TOY BOAT.
TOY BOAT.

WET WINTER WEATHER WITH WICKED WET WINDS.
WET WINTER WEATHER WITH WICKED WET WINDS.
WET WINTER WEATHER WITH WICKED WET WINDS.

HEARTY HEROES HIT HEAVY HENCHMEN.
HEARTY HEROES HIT HEAVY HENCHMEN.
HEARTY HEROES HIT HEAVY HENCHMEN.

J. JONAH JAMESON JUMPED JAUNTILY.
J. JONAH JAMESON JUMPED JAUNTILY.
J. JONAH JAMESON JUMPED JAUNTILY.

 STEVE SAVED SAILING SEALS SITTING SIDE BY SIDE.
STEVE SAVED SAILING SEALS SITTING SIDE BY SIDE.
STEVE SAVED SAILING SEALS SITTING SIDE BY SIDE.

 PEPPER POTTS PLACED PICKLED PEARS
ON THE PRETTY PERCH.
PEPPER POTTS PLACED PICKLED PEARS
ON THE PRETTY PERCH.
PEPPER POTTS PLACED PICKLED PEARS
ON THE PRETTY PERCH.

 CHOP SHOPS STOCK CHOPS.
CHOP SHOPS STOCK CHOPS.
CHOP SHOPS STOCK CHOPS.

 TONGUE
TWISTERS

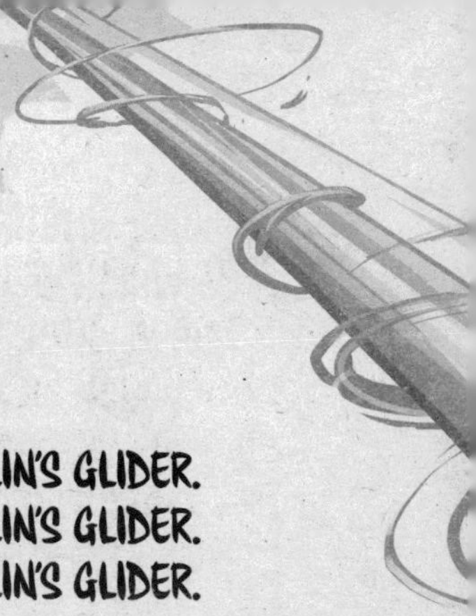

UNIQUE NEW YORK!
UNIQUE NEW YORK!
UNIQUE NEW YORK!

GREG GUARDED GREEN GOBLIN'S GLIDER.
GREG GUARDED GREEN GOBLIN'S GLIDER.
GREG GUARDED GREEN GOBLIN'S GLIDER.

TAMMY TRAINS TARANTULAS IN A TERRIBLE TENNESSEE TOWN. TRAIN, TAMMY, TRAIN!
TAMMY TRAINS TARANTULAS IN A TERRIBLE TENNESSEE TOWN. TRAIN, TAMMY, TRAIN!
TAMMY TRAINS TARANTULAS IN A TERRIBLE TENNESSEE TOWN. TRAIN, TAMMY, TRAIN!

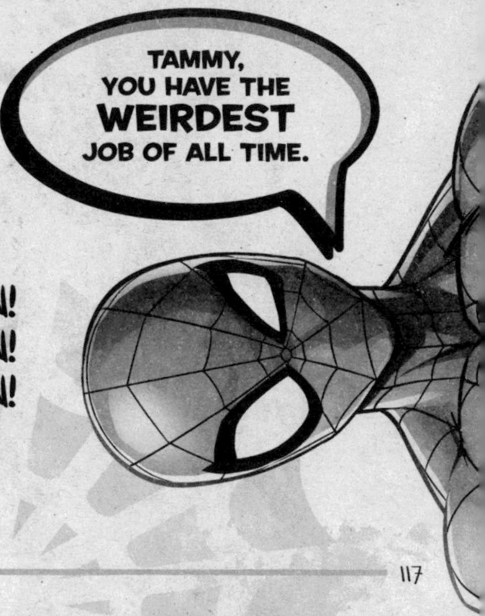
TAMMY, YOU HAVE THE WEIRDEST JOB OF ALL TIME.

STUPID SUPERSTITION!
STUPID SUPERSTITION!
STUPID SUPERSTITION!

WISE WITCHES WISH WEIRD WISHES.
WHICH WEIRD WISHES DID WISE WITCHES WISH?
WISE WITCHES WISH WEIRD WISHES.
WHICH WEIRD WISHES DID WISE WITCHES WISH?
WISE WITCHES WISH WEIRD WISHES.
WHICH WEIRD WISHES DID WISE WITCHES WISH?

VULTURE VOWED: "A VALIANT VACATION!"
VULTURE VOWED: "A VALIANT VACATION!"
VULTURE VOWED: "A VALIANT VACATION!"

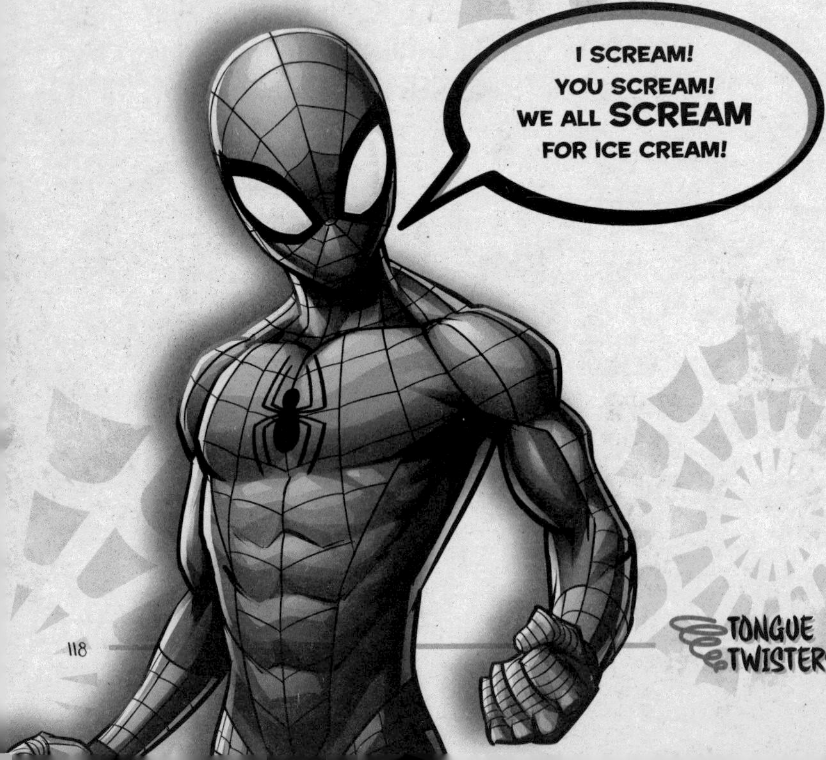
I SCREAM!
YOU SCREAM!
WE ALL SCREAM
FOR ICE CREAM!

Spider-Man ● @WallCrawlerNYC
So bored sitting on the top of this bank.
DRAMATIC SIGH. I hope a scientist with
octopus tentacles doesn't try to steal all
the $$$ inside.

 Spider-Man ● @WallCrawlerNYC
Now it's raining! Webbed up a little
umbrella. Feelin' cozy. Oh no. I feel pigeons
on top of it. Or as I like to call them, DEMON
SKY RATS!

 Spider-Man ● @WallCrawlerNYC
GAH! The pigeons are ATTACKING me! I
REPEAT, THE PIGEONS ARE ATTACKING ME!
Someone call for help! Uh-oh. Bank alarm
going off. BRB

 Spider-Man ● @WallCrawlerNYC
Robbery = foiled by ME. YOU'RE WELCOME,
NYC. Dumb ol' Doc Ock read my tweet and
fell for my trap. What a bonehead. Gonna
go nap. Laterz!

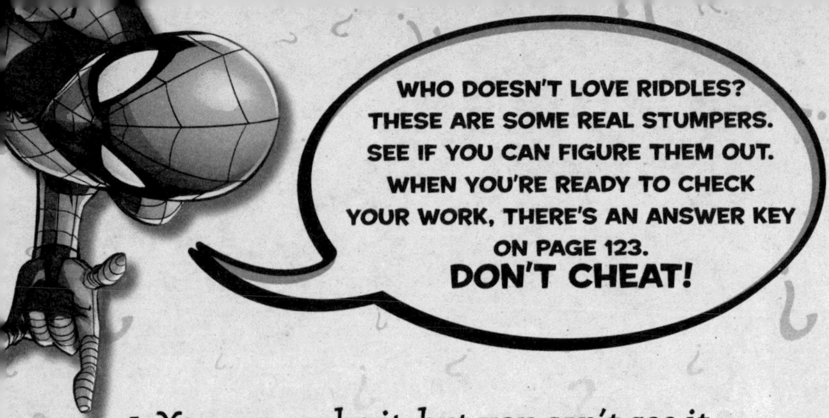
WHO DOESN'T LOVE RIDDLES? THESE ARE SOME REAL STUMPERS. SEE IF YOU CAN FIGURE THEM OUT. WHEN YOU'RE READY TO CHECK YOUR WORK, THERE'S AN ANSWER KEY ON PAGE 123.
DON'T CHEAT!

1. You can make it, but you can't see it. What is it?

2. Poor people have it. Rich people need it. If you eat it, you die. What is it?

3. What can you catch but not throw?

4. It is as light as a feather, but most people are unable to hold it for more than a minute. What is it?

5. What has a neck but no head?

6. Scott's father had three sons: Alex, Gabriel, and . . . ?

7. What word is spelled incorrectly in every dictionary?

8. What has one eye but can't see?

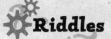

9. If I have it, I don't share it. If I share it, I don't have it. What is it?

10. What can you hold but never touch?

11. How much dirt is in a hole that's twelve feet deep and five feet wide?

12. There was a ship filled with people, but there wasn't a single person on the ship. Why?

Riddles

ANSWER KEY

1. Noise.

2. Nothing.

3. A cold.

4. Their breath.

5. A bottle.

6. Scott.

7. Incorrectly.

8. A needle.

9. A secret.

10. A conversation.

11. None. It's a hole.

12. They were all married.

SOOOO, HOW'D YOU DO?

Riddles

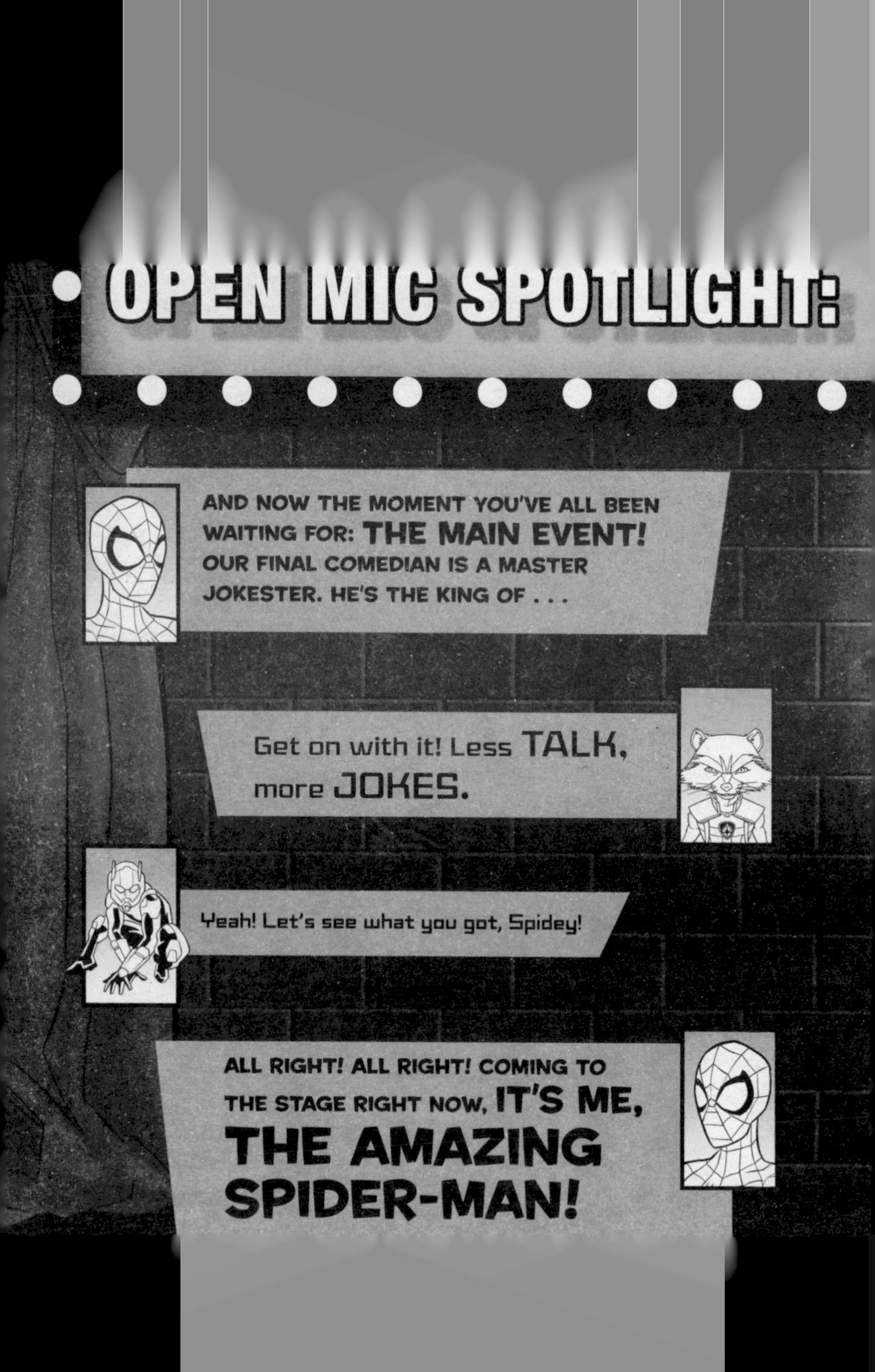
OPEN MIC SPOTLIGHT:
AND NOW THE MOMENT YOU'VE ALL BEEN WAITING FOR: THE MAIN EVENT! OUR FINAL COMEDIAN IS A MASTER JOKESTER. HE'S THE KING OF . . .
Get on with it! Less TALK, more JOKES.
Yeah! Let's see what you got, Spidey!
ALL RIGHT! ALL RIGHT! COMING TO THE STAGE RIGHT NOW, IT'S ME, THE AMAZING SPIDER-MAN!

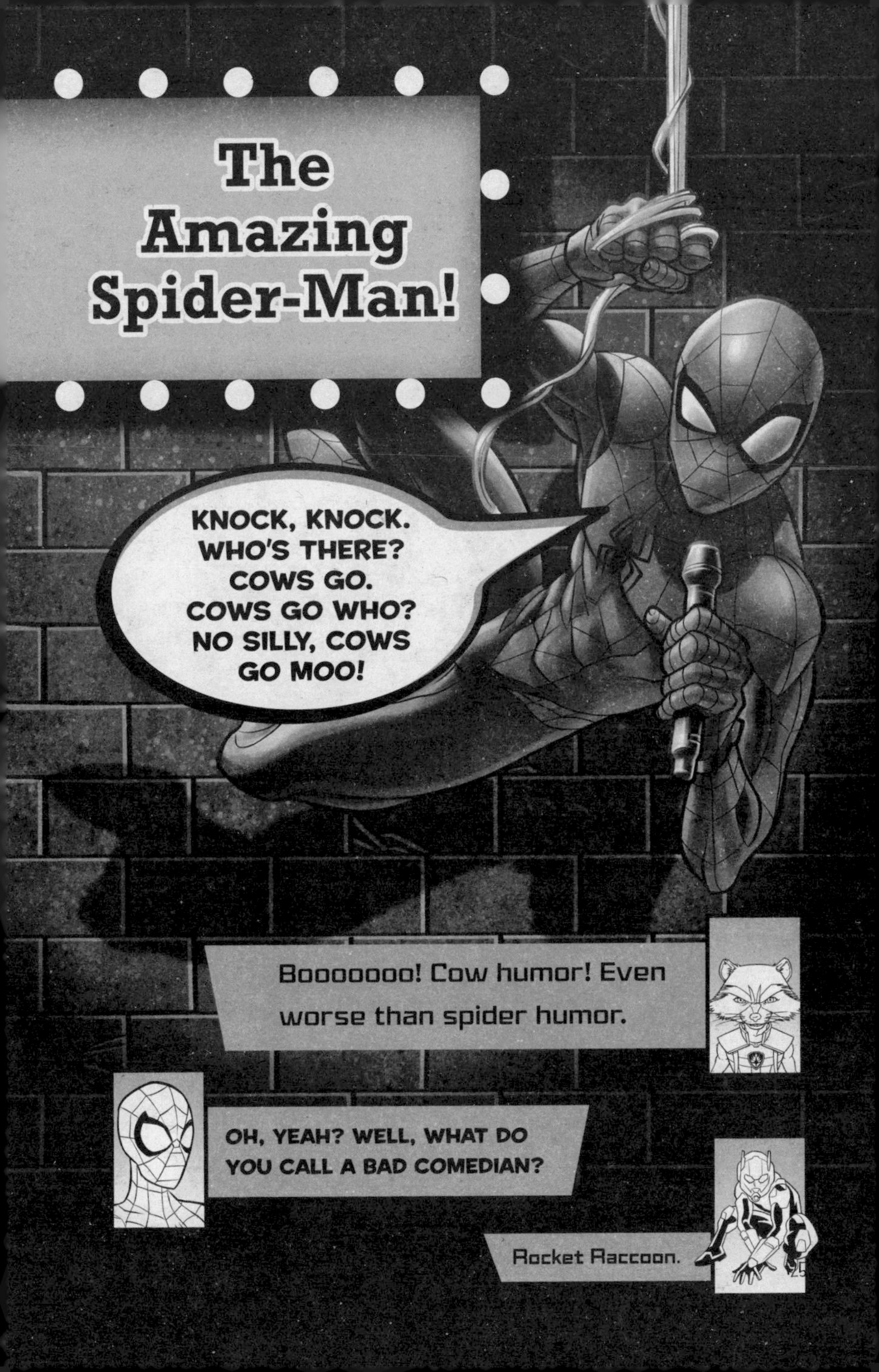
The Amazing Spider-Man!
KNOCK, KNOCK. WHO'S THERE? COWS GO. COWS GO WHO? NO SILLY, COWS GO MOO!
Booooooo! Cow humor! Even worse than spider humor.
OH, YEAH? WELL, WHAT DO YOU CALL A BAD COMEDIAN?
Rocket Raccoon.

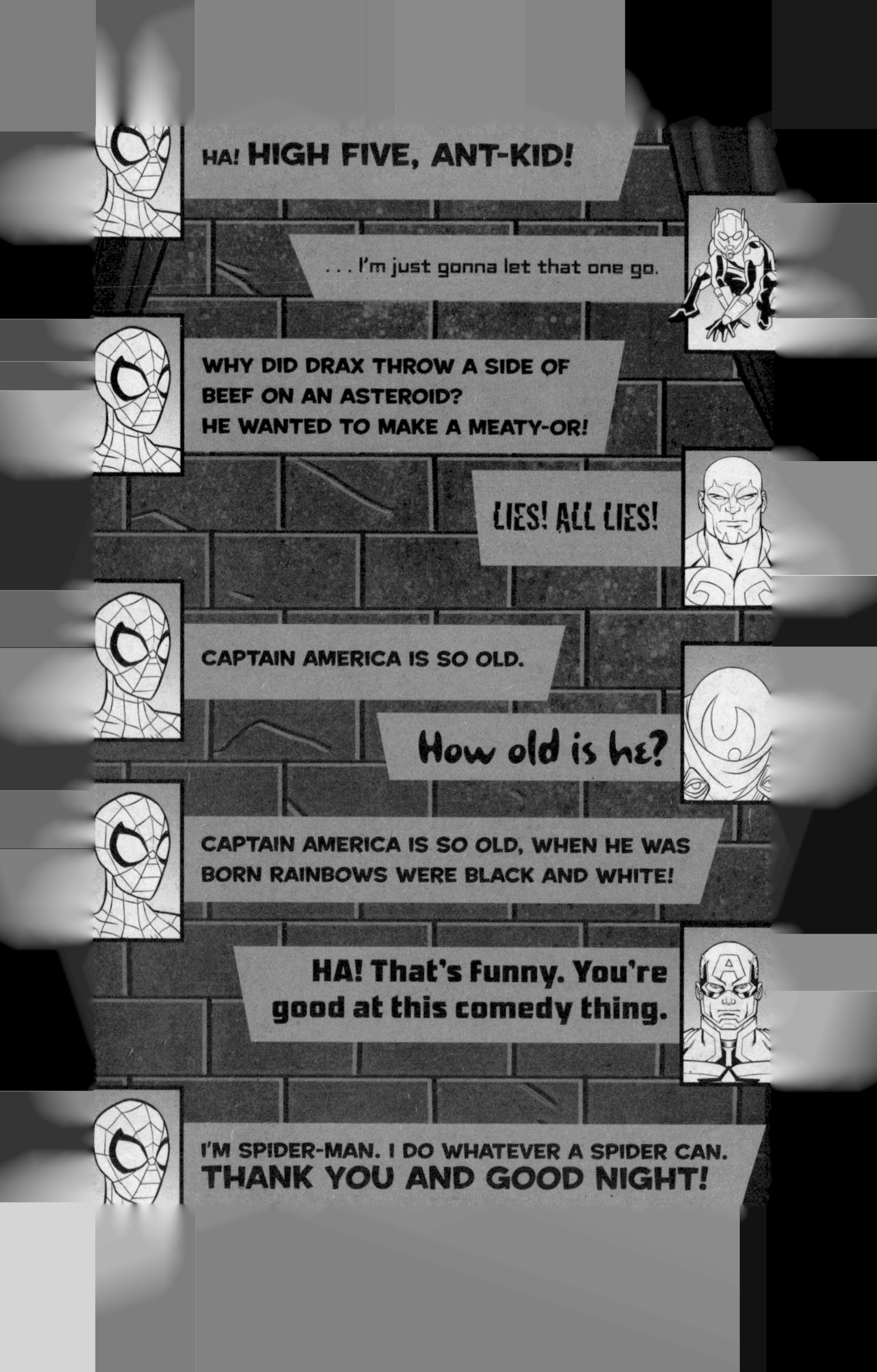

HA! HIGH FIVE, ANT-KID!
. . . I'm just gonna let that one go.
WHY DID DRAX THROW A SIDE OF BEEF ON AN ASTEROID? HE WANTED TO MAKE A MEATY-OR!
LIES! ALL LIES!
CAPTAIN AMERICA IS SO OLD.
How old is he?
CAPTAIN AMERICA IS SO OLD, WHEN HE WAS BORN RAINBOWS WERE BLACK AND WHITE!
HA! That's funny. You're good at this comedy thing.
I'M SPIDER-MAN. I DO WHATEVER A SPIDER CAN. THANK YOU AND GOOD NIGHT!

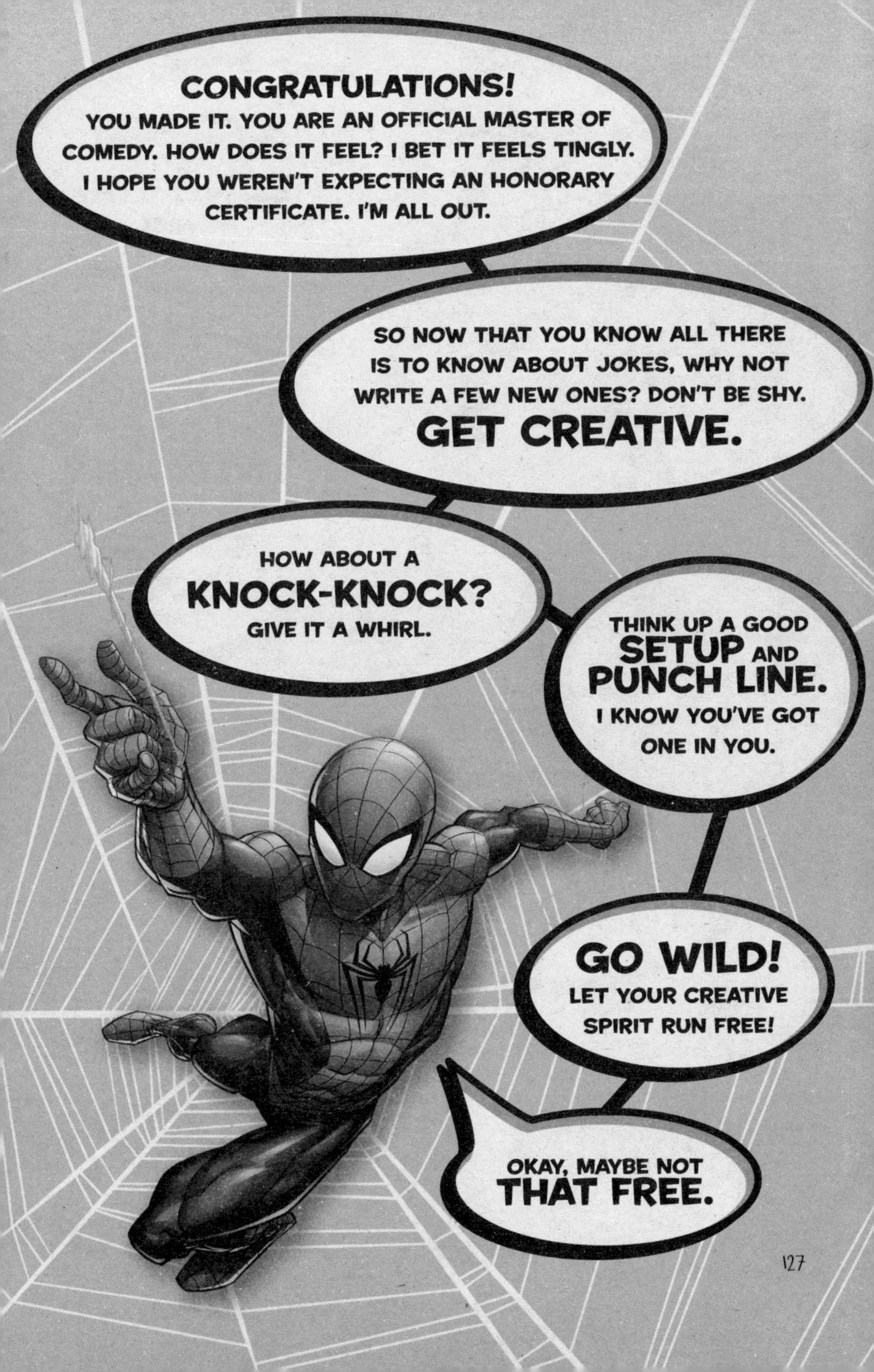
CONGRATULATIONS!
YOU MADE IT. YOU ARE AN OFFICIAL MASTER OF COMEDY. HOW DOES IT FEEL? I BET IT FEELS TINGLY. I HOPE YOU WEREN'T EXPECTING AN HONORARY CERTIFICATE. I'M ALL OUT.
SO NOW THAT YOU KNOW ALL THERE IS TO KNOW ABOUT JOKES, WHY NOT WRITE A FEW NEW ONES? DON'T BE SHY. GET CREATIVE.
HOW ABOUT A KNOCK-KNOCK? GIVE IT A WHIRL.
THINK UP A GOOD SETUP AND PUNCH LINE. I KNOW YOU'VE GOT ONE IN YOU.
GO WILD! LET YOUR CREATIVE SPIRIT RUN FREE!
OKAY, MAYBE NOT THAT FREE.

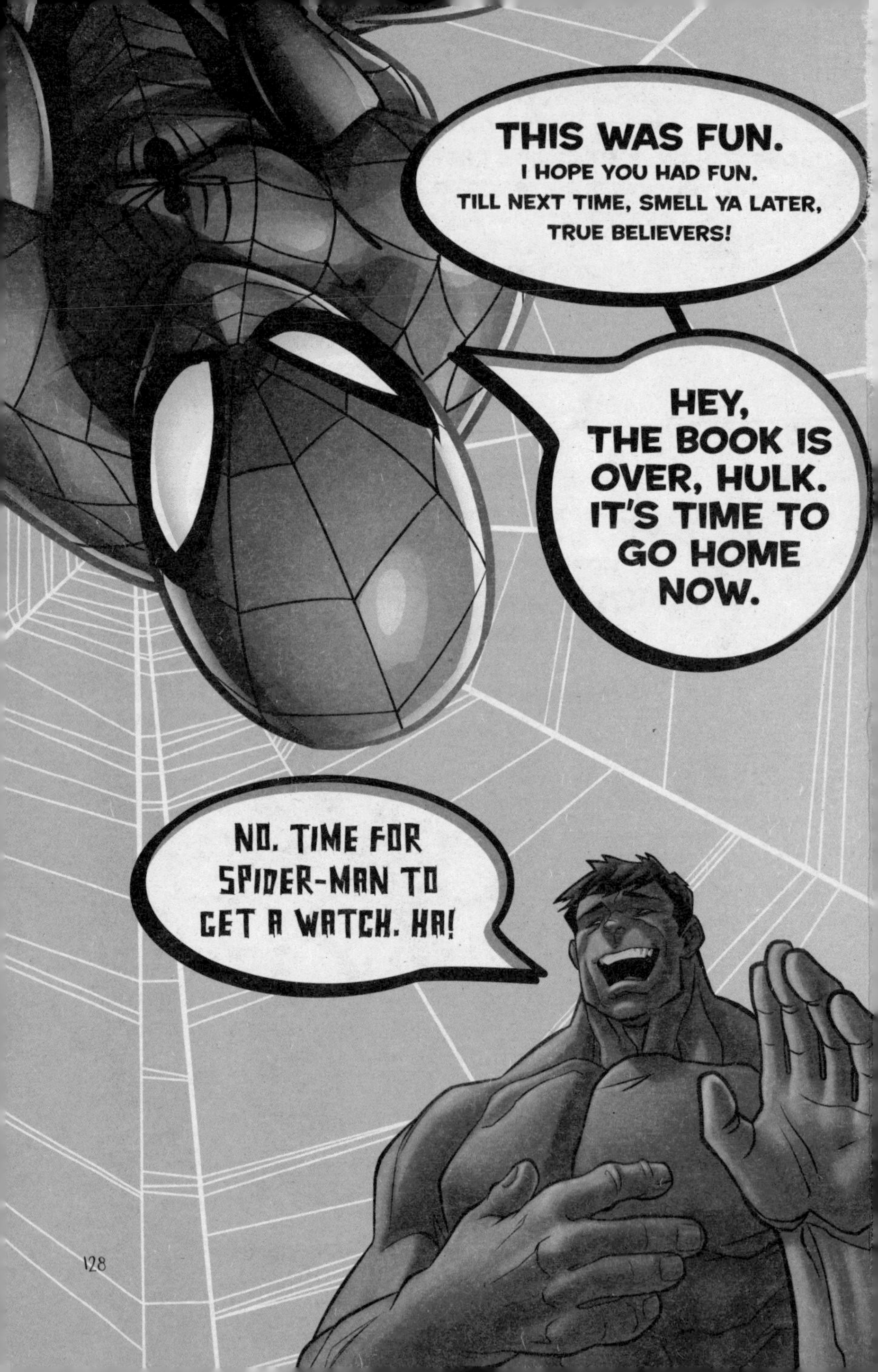
THIS WAS FUN.
I HOPE YOU HAD FUN.
TILL NEXT TIME, SMELL YA LATER,
TRUE BELIEVERS!
HEY, THE BOOK IS OVER, HULK. IT'S TIME TO GO HOME NOW.
NO. TIME FOR SPIDER-MAN TO GET A WATCH. HA!